"fools say"

BY THE SAME AUTHOR

Translator of all the above works: Maria Jolas

a novel by
Nathalie Sarraute

"fools
say"

TRANSLATED BY
MARIA JOLAS

GEORGE BRAZILLER
NEW YORK

Originally published in France under the title
    "Disent les imbéciles"
    © 1976, by Editions Gallimard

Library of Congress Cataloging in Publication Data

Sarraute, Nathalie.
    "Fools say".

    Translation of "Disent les imbéciles".
    I.   Title.
PZ4.S2488Fo   [PQ2637.A783]   843'.9'14   76–16696
ISBN 0–8076–0837–8

First Printing

Printed in the United States of America

She's sweet, isn't she?   Just look at that...
Look how fine it is...   you'd never think it was
real hair, it's like feathers, or down...   their
fingers caress the silken, slightly wrinkled skin of
her cheek...   her tender flesh yields docilely under their pressure...   moving down the length of
her shoulder under a downy white scarf, they
come to rest on her rather puffy hands, dotted
with little gold spots, which she is holding motionless on her knees...   she nods with an air of
tender indulgence, smiles her nice innocent
smile, nothing penetrates, no "piercing" glance
comes through the gleaming enamel of her eyes...
    She is sweet...   the soft, fragile skin of her
limp cheeks, when you graze them with your
finger tips, gives you a feeling...   you feel like
holding your breath...   your fingers begin to
roam, they follow the outlines of her skull which

has retained all its roundness under the thin covering of lustrous hair... she is sweet... so frail, so docile... their fingers gently grip her shoulders, her arm under the frothy scarf, their rounded palms encompass the soft cushions shot through with little bluish veins dotted with spots, that swell the back of her hands... She is sweet... couldn't you just bite her...

—But what's happening? They straighten up, they remove their hands... What's the matter with you?

—Nothing. Leave her alone, that's all. Don't touch her.

—But you yourself a while ago...

—Yes, that's true, I shouldn't have. I let myself be taken in... But after all, I'm too stupid... Well, I think I'll leave...

But it's too late. You can't get out of it that easily. Don't let him go, he must answer... he let himself be taken in by what? What's got into you? When you start, you must go all the way to the end.

To the end, really? To the end with you... You want to see how far... and you are ready to follow me... Not to the end, of course... which end? what pretension... but just a short way? You will? That doesn't

make you afraid?   And suppose you were in-
duced to take part in something you preferred to
have nothing to do with, which ordinarily you
would have the good taste, the sense of propriety
to ignore...   Suppose you were about to commit
yourself?   Be subjected to certain contacts?

Afraid?   He really has lost his mind.
Afraid, us!   We accomplices.   Contacts with us.
What contacts, I ask you, what other contacts
than the unavoidable brushings between a rascal
who disturbs the peace and the police officer who
leads him away, their wrists chained to each
other.
Impossible now for you to get out of it.
A border has been crossed.   Words have been
spoken.   An act has been committed.   You have
broken the law.

He should be arrested, he should be inter-
rogated...   gently at first, so as not to inhibit him.
We'll have to start with a quick re-enactment.
Everything will have to be shown again as it happened.   If you want, let's see, let's take a look
together.
Here, then, is a blue velvet couch...
the blue she loves...   that matches the enamel of
her eyes.   Who is seated on the couch?   Reply...
—What's the good?   You know it.   —We know

it, but it is indispensable for her to be named.
—Her name is Cyprienne. —Then what?
—Cyprienne Létuvier. —Oh the little rascal,
the slyboots, he smelt the danger, he saw the
trap... Don't try to get around it... There's no
question of her last name, or of her first name,
but of what she is to us, which you know.
Yes, of what she stands for to each one of us.
—She's... she's our grandmother...

Good. That settles the first point.
It had to be said. So our grandmother was
seated on her couch, surrounded by us. And we
were cajoling her and you were caressing her and
we couldn't take our eyes off of her sweet faded
face, we were lightly stroking, with what precau-
tions, her very fine hair... like down... her
cheeks with skin that is the silkiest, satiniest...
we laid our hands, pressed our lips, on the little
cushions of her hands, our fingers followed the
outlines of her veins, blue-tinted, like the faded
enamel of her eyes... her quiet hands resting on
her spread knees between which her soft woolen
skirt made a hollow... a refuge for our heads to
snuggle in... yes, her hands, the slightest detail
of which I am familiar with... on this finger, the
ring finger, there is a little hollow at the height of
the knuckle, like a tiny crater, which the tip of my
index finger recognizes when it barely grazes the
slightly puffy, rounded edges... Stop fiddling
with her like that, you'll tire her... That's not
true, is it? No, we're not tiring you... she nods,

she gives us one of her nice smiles. How sweet she is... couldn't you just bite her...

This was when it seized him all of a sudden, he couldn't contain himself, he straightened up, he shouted... and now he's afraid, he's ashamed, look at him, he's hiding his face in his hands, passing his fingers over his forehead, stroking it, to restore order in that crazy, reckless head... It's madness, I know... forgive me, pay no attention, let's consider that I said nothing... nothing... there is nothing, I'm mad...

"Mad? Really mad? Are you certain of that? Is it that sure?"... a sort of hiss, a barely perceptible whistle... emanating from there, from the one who had never stopped observing everything with the look, the smile, of a certain connivance, a slightly mocking, amused complicity...

Ah, so you too, you sensed all that the way I did... One single witness is enough, a single one who also... I am not mad... you murmured it to me, I heard you whisper: "Is it that sure? Really mad?"... You understood everything, I knew that, while we were caressing her, while our hands were holding her close, molding her contours, checking them... you were amused, still a bit remote... Still safe...

No? You didn't see anything? You didn't whisper anything? Those were hallucinations... pure madness... I apologize, I was in the wrong... Caress, cajole her as much as you like. I don't know what got into me... what I could have been thinking of...

But proofs exist, in the face of which there's nothing you can do... You straightened up, you looked at us with an expression of disgust, you dared to insinuate goodness knows what... we know you, you stop at nothing... You were foolish enough to set into motion our defense system. Numerous refined, graduated measures, adapted to each case. Now you know what to expect.

There's no use trying to vindicate yourself, the facts are obvious. There we all were together, making a charming family picture. Nothing in the world more moving. A delicious grandmother, a real grandmamma, like the ones in fairy tales... it was very fortunate for us... seated in her favorite place, surrounded by her grandchildren... they kiss her, cajole her, they reverently stroke her silken hair, in which strains that are still golden mingle with white... they lay their fingers on the dimples of her chubby hands, and she lets them do so, she smiles as she nods her head... isn't she sweet? couldn't you just bite her? But suddenly you straightened up, it was more than you could stand... You shouted, hands off, will you leave her alone, you who were

there as we were, more than us, caressing her...
Let her alone...   and then, no, I think I'll leave.

There, there, never mind, that's what we
need, everything is foreseen, the rule and the
exceptions, nothing new under the sun, everything is known, classified, woefully monotonous,
and nothing is clearer, nothing has been more
seriously analyzed, than his case.

That's what we want; that, all of a sudden,
is what will follow the meanderings, flow into all
the bends, hunt down in every recess, breathe in,
collect in a single block and bring to light what
was there, scattered: caresses, tenderness, rever-
ent touching, head snuggled between knees, sudden tongue-lashing, hate-filled glances, all collected together in those two words, there, staring
us in the face: he's jealous.

There it is, the easiest weapon to handle,
the most effective one in their arsenal.   This is
the one, he knew it, that they would immediately
bring out and aim at him.   There is nothing
more astonishing than the rapidity, the force with
which this word strikes, penetrates, spreads...

And yet it is a word which doesn't look like
much, an apparently perfectly harmless word
with its "jeal" that consolidates, and its "ous"
that unites, "ous" like "us"... But you can't

count on this, there's nothing trickier than these sound effects... Remember we have "jeal" for "jel," "ous" for "us." It's all there, in the unpronounced letters, in the "a" and the "o." That makes all the difference. And the barely uttered, intimate "ous" coupled with the confidently accentuated "jeal," gives something that, in a twinkling, produces transformations that... No computer in a million years will ever come up with what we know takes place in each one of us as soon as that word "jealous" is spoken... who could ever develop it, enlarge or extend it... And what would be the use? It's enough to say he's "jealous." At once, without his knowing why, without his being able to explain why, the enormous machinery that is as complicated as the one that makes our lungs breathe, or our pulse beat, makes his blood rush to his head, his face grows red... "Jealous? Me!"

There he is running away while they laugh, there he is trembling, struggling... How funny he looks... We see his back rise up and make ripples in the blanket we threw over him to catch him... Look at him, I am holding him in the hollow of my hand, the better for you to examine him... his grim look, fleeing ours... You don't know where to hide, you'd like to be a thousand leagues under the earth, wouldn't you, when you've been caught in the act... What act?...

14

Do you hear his pitiful little cries? What act? Need it be explained? There we were all together. A delightful picture. Our grandmother, and all of us gathered about her cajoling, caressing her, snuggling our faces in the hollow of her soft skirt... All united in the same tenderness, all huddled up in the same security... and he alone, while, like us, he tenderly laid his fingers on her silky hair, on her cheek...

He alone... turncoat, he alone traitor, entrenched within himself, greedy, full of hatred... —Hatred, you think so? Yes, hatred, that's well-known. You're never jealous of people you like. That's been analyzed, the best minds have noticed it. I read... —You're right, I read it too, in Spinoza. —Spinoza? Oh, well,... You know me, I never went that far... But since Spinoza... Yes, no jealousy without hatred. They're twins. And in fact, he looked daggers of hatred, disgust and repulsion when one of us... —But you saw how he too, like us, he said it too, I heard him... —Of course, but he can take that liberty... he can say "she's sweet," he can cajole her, she belongs to him. But for us, when we dared to touch his possession, his exclusive property...

All at once, he extricates, frees himself... There... I've got it... Thanks... That was what I needed... You see you discovered it, without knowing what you were doing, you touched it... "His possession, his property"... do it again, just a little better, you're hot, go ahead, say it, say: "Yes, his thing"... —Yes, your thing... —Thanks for giving it to me... thing... Thing is just the word. A word that says everything.

A thing, you saw that. An object, set there before us, on display, for disposal... Her soft hair, her silky cheeks, the sparkling enamel of her eyes, the dimples in her plump hands lying on her knees, on her skirt with its soft folds...

You're right, it will have to be reenacted... Our fingers were following her contours, our eyes were gazing at her coloring... delicate pastel pinks and blues... her indulgent nod, her innocent smile... "She is sweet." Each word— marvellous. "She is sweet."

But don't be afraid... Don't look at me like that... I'm not mad... He's right, that one over there, watching me with a sneer... wondering how far I'll go... Not far, you may be sure, not very far, I'm too weak, too timorous, just a few steps...

"Look how sweet she is." To begin with "She," anonymous, she, which can mean just anybody, she, a word that sets her at a distance, a little lower down. "She"... But why insist? That, you've been taught, without any explanations, any reasons having been given you, it would be too complicated, too much of a task, to remember them... "She," forbidden in her presence, that's all, according to our customs. And very wise they are.

Now it's the turn of "is." "Is," which cements, petrifies... "is," which blocks all exits. Impossible to escape from it... "Is"... but you know it... And now the pearl, now the best of all: "sweet"... Little piece of Dresden china on the mantelpiece, Tanagra statuette, enchanting doll... But what's the use? Everyone feels it and you felt it... "She is sweet. Couldn't you just bite her?" Bite her. Bite her. Then came the crack-up.

But that's not entirely true. That didn't come until just now. At the time, there was not exactly a crack-up, it was more of a ripple, an undulation, a waver... In her opaque eyes, in back of the bright reflections, something moved... She's sweet, couldn't you just bite her... That was going a bit too far, under the pressure of what was crushing her, something stirred, gave an ultimate start...

Then, on the spot where the rising begins, where it ripples, on that little swelling, that unevenness, there is where I seized it between my fingers and pulled, tearing off everything, the entire stage curtain, and through this enormous hole... it poured forth, a boiling mass, it kept on flowing, dragging me along with it...

Stop that... Help... Put up partitions, separate, shut in what is running from her, spreading... stop it... You have everything you need to channel it, capture it, overpower it, all your categories, all your psychology... quick, let's dam, enclose, orient, bring on the specially created words, intended for this purpose... here they are, let's take them: revolt, repressed needs, live desires, as alive as formerly, renunciations, rancors, furors, mutilations, little acts of cowardice, hypocrisy, fearlessness, malice, kindness, naïveté, clearsightedness, sensuality... There, little by little the flood is calming down, I am calming down... The crisis has passed.

It is soothing to use these partitions to put everything back in place, to separate and stow away in different compartments, in properly labeled drawers... You have only to open them, it's there, known, classified. One can amuse oneself by taking this one here and another one there and making subtle mixtures for delicate tastes; match tenderness with rancor, vindictiveness with generosity... exquisite compositions... So many subtle minds are past masters at it... so many masterpieces have shown admired models of what can be made out of these

sophisticated mixtures, these assemblages simi-
lar to the ones made of bits of cloth with which
women used to make those multicolored quilts
that are so pleasantly effective, and appear to be
so modern.

No? You don't like that? You disap-
prove of it? This pretty counterpane made of
clashing pieces is not to your taste. You miss
the old painted stuffs. And yet you'll admit that
they were a bit outmoded, rather insipid...
Look at her, isn't she a bit cloying?...

For a moment they remain motionless,
eyes staring, as though in a daze... and then
they begin to make excited gestures... They
clasp him, they crush him, their hard fingers dig
into his shoulders, their hands seize his head
from behind and hold it... You can be satisfied.
It was insipid for your taste, insipid to the point
of disgust? You wanted to make it spicy.
But look what you've made of it... how everything is hardening, reassuming form... Look,
there it is, evident... it's no longer insipid, far
from it... you can't complain any more. What
could be less insipid than that? This old woman
with a dubiously pink, slightly bluish face, in
which only the eyes have retained... or perhaps
acquired... they didn't have it... the glitter...
the shine... a sort of glint that is... Give me the
word, hand it to me... Yes, that's it... libidi-

nous... a libidinous glint... Don't struggle, hold him tight, pull up his eyelids so he can't close them... yes, libidinous... Surrounded by her wrinkles, that glint, through an effect of perfectly natural contrast, appears to be... libidinous is the word... look at the flabby folds of that gamy flesh underneath which unmentionable desires are coiled... those thin, receding lips... that disheveled gray hair of an old shrew, an old witch... because she can be pretty savage, our good grandmother can, we had forgotten that... Look at her clawlike fingers, you remember them? That comes back to me now, those little scratches which, all at once, when you least expected it, she knew how to give... He is growing restless, he shouts, tears are streaming from his staring eyes... He is struggling to attack what they have erected before him, to destroy it...
—That's not true, that's a lie... You can't live unless you're surrounded by fakes. Everything you do is faked. I won't allow it, you haven't the right, you are filthy...

—Filthy? Us? That's really perfect... We filthy. But if you could see yourself... If you could see those feverish eyes, that curve of your lips in which something cold, mean...
—Cold... Mean? When, on the contrary, I tried to liberate her from the spell that had been cast over her, and which had changed her into that little old woman, whereas in her, as formerly, as in each one of us, as strongly as ever, we are

the same... when I ran the risk, a deadly risk, as you see... when I exposed myself... —Yes, exposed, that's true, exposed is the word, you showed yourself as you are. They beat him on the chest, on the forehead... It was oozing from everywhere:˙ coldness. Icy curiosity. Clear-sightedness without pity. Without love. Do you want her to see your unvarnished self? Do you want us to tell her?...

He is leaning toward her, she is seated straight upright on her couch, her opaque, gleaming eyes, traversed by no piercing glance, are turned on him... In back of them, how-ever... or is it merely a reflection of those bril-liant enameled surfaces?... it is as though some-thing had moved, a movement like that of a little frightened animal, burrowing, fleeing... She smiles at him, her gentle innocent smile, she lays her hand on his head which he is hiding in the hollow of her downy skirt, she is caressing his hair... he's her big crazy boy, her big stupid... poor child, life will make him suffer, sensitive and affectionate as he is. Her little chick. Her little Tom Thumb. Always looking for the pebbles on his road, to go where, I ask you... always racking his brain, always haunted by the idea of doing wrong... Who among us has forgotten his bloodstained hands, the day he almost slashed his wrists when he broke a windowpane to free a

duck marked for slaughter by old Marie...
the kind old woman was very upset... he had
always been her favorite... Kindness itself.
He hasn't changed, people don't change...
She nods her head... Certainly not, they don't
tire her, on the contrary... but he's always
afraid, he's the most affectionate of them all, the
one who's the most attached to her... jealous,
yes, perhaps a little, they always teased him about
that... they're right, he doesn't like the others to
touch her, he wants her all to himself, a bit jealous, that's true, too ardent, but with a heart of
gold. And generous. He'd give you the shirt
off his back. And there's nothing he would not
do for her.

As her hand caresses him everything in
him softens, relaxes, all his wrinkles are ironed
out, all his creases erased... He fixes on her the
gaze that she loves, his frank gaze, his confident
childlike gaze that slips and slides over her
slightly made-up pink face, over her unobtru-
sively rouged lips, over her hair in which gold and
silver threads mingle, over her hands resting quietly on her knees... her entire self becoming visible, gathered together, there, in this face, in
these hands... Sheltered. Secure. In this haven that she has entered, to which, without ever
attempting to take flight, to set out for the open
sea, before she is even headed towards it, before
she is summoned to take refuge in it, she has
prudently repaired, wisely to settle down among

22

the old training ships, these fine old sailing vessels that people visit with emotion, with respect.

What does he want?   Where does he want to take her, take them both, this crazy boy of hers, her big stupid?   Towards what terrible dangers, what nightmares, what horrors...   Toward what mental hospitals in which society confines overexcited old women with disheveled gray hair, libidinous old hags, their eyes flushed with desire, their grotesquely threatening gnarled fists, toward what reformatory where awful scoundrels, gallows birds, contemptible little rascals are kept...

—Yes, like you...   Shall we tell you, what this little sweetheart, this innocent babe murmured, what this angel-face has got on his mind, what is oozing from his nice, frank gaze?

—Nothing, don't believe them...   it's not true, they are the ones, as soon as I tried to rescue you from this form you're confined in, to free you from that evil spell...   they were the ones... if you knew, if you had heard their sneers: Ah, "she's sweet" isn't suitable?   "she's sweet" isn't respectful?...

—Yes, he explained it to us.   Would you like us to repeat it to her?...   But what's the use, she would not understand, she, thank goodness, in spite of her age, has retained all her faculties...   Indeed; you'll see, let's try...   —No, be quiet...

—No we won't, it'll be interesting... So tell us, grandmamma... you know how much he likes for people to speak frankly, to leave nothing unsaid, to have things out between adults, between people who like each other, you know him, those are his own expressions... "She is sweet," would you believe it, he was shocked by that... he sensed that under this blow, under this pressure, you were struggling, he sensed that in back of those enamel-blue eyes that we so love, there was something... —No, be quiet... —He did too, something that was hiding, something... But he should show it, for us such things as that, fortunately for us, fortunately for everybody, we don't see them...

Now don't get so excited... We just wanted to frighten you... How could you expect us to dare let her know?... What do you take us for? No, don't tremble, we're just going to ask her, put a question to her that she'll be capable of answering: So tell us, dear grandmamma, did we annoy you the least bit, did you think it was too familiar on our part, when we caressed your hair, as soft as down, the silky skin of your cheek... Did you think it was insolent of us to say: "Look how sweet she is, couldn't you just bite her?" Did "she's sweet" shock you?

She nods her head, turns on him a slightly sorrowful, fond look... Surely that's just another one of his ideas... What's this invention of his? What has he discovered now by dint of sheer delicacy, consideration?... What is there in these words except the affectionate familiarity that she has always loved in her grandchildren, except that flavor of childhood, of their childhood, that the word "sweet" gave to her pink and blue face, to her gold and silver hair, to her chubby hands, to her fluffy shawl, to her skirt with its soft folds, as though they had been chosen on purpose and deposited, indelibly imprinted in them, intended reverently to be kept there... In him too, isn't that so? she does not want him to lack for that... He is not going to renounce his share of what she will leave them all, renounce this gift? Will he? He is not ungrateful, is he? Not irreverent? For nothing in the world would he dare to neglect, profane... She knows him... His frank gaze, his cool, smooth little hand, caress her, his greedy child's lips come nearer, form a circle: "How sweet she is"...

"She's sweet." A piece of sugar candy. A caramel flavored with sweet fruit, with honey, delicious to suck, to let it soften in your mouth, to pull... she's sweet... an unctuous pasty substance... What's it made of? Nothing that isn't perfectly wholesome, articles of the best quality: "She," the familiarity of which lends zest to that tenderness, that respect...

"Is"—a currently employed ingredient which people use without thinking, actually they could do without it, but why deprive themselves of it?   it's perfectly harmless, tasteless, flavor-less, and so convenient for thickening...

"Sweet"...   but what is it?   it's not candy, not fruit paste, I can't chew it, I take it out of my mouth all wet and shiny...   It's the luck-charm, a tiny china doll...   it was my turn, I had that good fortune, I found it in my piece of the birthday cake...

Who? Who is it? Who is he? From the moment he made his appearance, they have never ceased to examine him impatiently, to scrutinize him... Let's hold him up to the light, consider him from all angles... the signs are still faint, there's little so far to get your teeth in, but for the time being we'll have to be satisfied with what we have: a high forehead, the forehead of a thinker, a mouth that gives evidence of firmness, a chin... Isn't there in that chin?... No, you'll see, it's a chin which, as it develops, will indicate will power, virility, because when it comes to being virile, ah, you can say what you like, he's a real boy, and at the same time, look at those long lashes, it's even a shame, what a waste, when so many girls... and those hands... have you noticed his long, tapering pianist's fingers... Yes, there's no doubt about it, you have immense luck, he's a gift from heaven, a real treasure.

And he blind, deaf, unaware, as on the day when they will wash him, dress him, lay him on his back, fold his hands on his chest, surround him with flowers, gaze at his high forehead from which the wrinkles have disappeared... How young he looks, those well-drawn lips, that wilful chin, those closed eyelids bordered with long lashes... Really he never looked handsomer.

But why hark so far back, why look so far ahead, why go to such extremes? From one end of the trajectory to the other, their gaze has never ceased to skim over him, the inaudible murmur surrounding him has never ceased.

It is as though a tacit countersign circulated among them, as though they had agreed among themselves to give him the feeling of not being seen, of not being remembered by them, of not being the subject of their conversations, never appearing in their dreams, their nightmares, so much so that he more than often has the reassuring impression of moving among them like the fairy-tale figure who wears a cap that makes him invisible.

And all at once these sudden awakenings... What happened? His protective cap has been pulled off... There he is, in view... he is wide-eyed...

What's that? that's not me... —Come, come, you don't recognize yourself? —Of course I do... I can make out my features, I have seen them reflected in mirrors, captured on photographs, but never have I seen... I have never imagined... Admit it's not a good likeness... —Not a good likeness? Why, on the contrary, there are few photographs of you to compare with the way this snapshot has seized... —Seized that? —How do you mean, that? —That curled up lip, that sidewise glance... Don't you think that it gives me a look... —What look? —I don't really know... a cruel, underhanded look...

He studies their faces anxiously... nothing in their eyes, in their amused, slightly mocking smiles... nothing, not a shade, not the faintest trace of mistrust, of repulsion... is it possible that they don't see?... Or perhaps they are so accustomed to see him with this expression... But then why, how does it happen that I don't frighten you? Don't you think that I have a sinister look there? The face of a buccaneer?

Their heads sink into their shoulders, they shiver very hard, they laugh... Ah, that's true, I always thought so, you have only to look at him, no need for photographs, he frightens me, you have only to see him, don't you think that he's someone you would not like to meet on a dark corner? And then they watch him in a serious, somewhat disturbed, surprised way... had they forgotten how sensitive he is, he doesn't understand the most innocent jokes... No doubt

29

about it, he's still the same, still determined to demean himself... to hurt himself... He would like for us to cheer him up, wouldn't he? for us to compliment him...

He feels spreading across his face a child-like smile... they like him, that's certain, they are his friends, they know him, they know that he is true blue, that he's good through and through, that he wouldn't hurt a fly... He nods, he smiles at them, he sighs softly... —How stupid you all are...

From their barely opened lips it issued... a murmur, a hardly perceptible whisper... —His chin is growing longer, yes, I'm afraid, he'll have an undershot jaw... —Ah, like Uncle Fran-çois... and they grew silent... A look, a sign exchanged between them must have put them on their guard, incited them to be prudent... Once more they have enveloped him in silence, once more they have put on the magic cap that gives him the feeling of not being seen, as though in place of his body, of his face, there were an empty space that their glances pass through, in which nothing hinders them... nothing comes from him reaches, or disturbs the calm, opaque surface of their eyes.

"His"... They look, they observe, situated at a good distance, a form that he can't see, in which he is imprisoned, enclosed, circumscribed, demarcated, separated, designated by that word that they apply to him: his.

Something has become detatched from what they see, something hard, percussive, a meteorite which has landed in them, has become embedded, producing that crackle, that whistling sound... "His jaw is stretching... An undershot jaw..."

On that head that he is now rigged up in, on that face of his, which is beginning to spread, like their faces, as everybody looks on, it is advancing, lengthening, a chin to which the word galosh[1] came and stuck... galosh, valosh, osh...

(1)—*menton en galoche:* Although for Larousse, in 1922, this was a *proéminent, long et recourbé* chin that, by 1959, had become simply *long, pointu* and *recourbé;* although for Harrap, it is either a "slipper chin" or an "undershot jaw," a recent abridged Oxford dictionary makes no mention of such a chin, and gives for "undershot" no other definition than one concerning a wheel, "worked by water running under it." As for Webster, a galosh is a galosh, a chin is a chin, and they never meet, even though we do learn in the same volume that "lower teeth which project like a bulldog's" can be called "undershot" (like a wheel?), and that a "person" may be said to have an "undershot" jaw. In 1934, a certain Ch. Petit, in an English-French dictionary, defined "undershot" as *mu en dessous.* So, convinced that this is an "all holds" conundrum, I have decided to cut the pear in two and call it both an undershot jaw and a galosh-shaped chin. Depending on one's love of antiquity, it is interesting to know that the Greeks wore a *Kapolous,* or "wooden-soled shoe, to keep their feet dry," which was the first definition of the French *galoche. Translator's note.*

In place. According to requirements. To the law. Nothing to find fault with. Nothing to say.

Look if you want. But you won't see anything that could interest you, the most meticulous customs officer will not be able to find anything that is not authorized, anything that could keep a person from passing calmly through the entrance gate.

His name. He heard it distinctly... His name, like the click of a trigger behind his back, followed by a volley of bird shot: "Not intelligent? Really? You think so?...   —I'm sure. Gifted, that's certain, but not intelligent. —Yes, perhaps, at bottom... He stops, he's shaking, his head is swimming, he's about to lose consciousness, fall down... and they catch him... —Ah, at last, he's waiting for us... Quitter, there, always in the clouds. It's all we can do to follow you, you run from us like a rabbit...

At the time, no pain, just that little weakness and a new, strange sensation, it must be this sensation that people lying helpless, with an injured spinal column, when they try to get up and realize that their usual reflexes have ceased functioning, that their legs are paralyzed... one of their vital points must have been affected...

The center. The secret spot where the General Staff is located and from where he, the Commander-in-Chief, all the maps spread out for him to see, examining the lay of the land, listening to reports, taking decisions, directing operations, a bomb hit it... he is thrown to the ground, his insignia torn off, he is shaken, obliged to get up and walk, pushed forward by blows from rifle butts, kicks, into the gray flock of the prisoners, all dressed alike, classified in the same category: fools.

Impossible to defend oneself, to counter-attack: he has been disarmed. Impossible to escape, there's no place to hide, wherever he goes he'll be caught.

And it started... a sort of dual personality... One part of himself, in an effort to survive, coming unattached, separating, crawling towards them... trying to pull himself up to their height, to see through their spectacles, to adapt... Yes, I see, I see very clearly... they are gifts. I am rather gifted... But as regards... yes, you're right. It's not what you might call intelligence... No... and yet I can't be mistaken for the others, the ones about whom they say... —Do listen to him, it's really a curious case... He himself acknowledges... It's interesting, it

would be worth examining more closely...
—So you see, my case is not a desperate one...
I could perhaps get a re-examination... perhaps
a rehabilitation? —Now see here, how could
you? The poor creature is trying to outwit us.
He repeats what we say like a parrot... —No,
that's not true, I have kept my distance ever since
I found out... That was a shock. A revela-
tion... But since... —How do you mean since?
—Since then, whenever I think, when I allow myself to judge... I tell myself, I tell myself: that
doesn't hold water... shortsighted, weak judgement... Necessarily, since I'm not intelligent.
So we have there, admit it, a bit of myself that has
been saved, a bit of live tissue that has been preserved, that it will be perhaps possible to culti-
vate, to develop, and with which I'll succeed in
getting rid of the rest... —That's really touching... It's rare, such modesty, such perspicacity... Such perspicacity? You too are beginning to make me anxious... How do you expect
it to be possible? Of course, if he's helped,
prodded, propped up by us, ruled by us, terror-
ized, without knowing why, by dint of repeating
without understanding it "I am not intelligent,"
he may succeed in persuading himself, in being
on his guard...

It appears, there, on the outside... and
then there, and again there... like little lights,

fires that flare up against the vast dark mass...
From one to the other a line runs... becomes
blurred... reappears... a still vague form is assuming shape... now it stands out more clearly...
—What are you doing? —Who?... —Why,
you... —Me? Ah, yes, I was not paying attention... —So you weren't, you were elsewhere...
Come to... You know what you were doing
then? You know what that's called? —I was
looking... you understand... there and there...
sort of bright dots... and from one to the other...
—That's just what we were telling you: you were
thinking, just imagine... You were following
your idea, that's what it's called... You liked it,
didn't you? You admired it? Come, now,
don't deny it, you appeared fascinated, quite
blissful... —That is to say, it had seemed to
me... —Of course, it's cruelty to insist... in this
meagre, flat world in which he is confined...
in the kingdom of the blind... a little idea, just
his size... there's a shoe for every foot...
his poor malformed foot... His little brain from
which ideas always issue defenseless... His
brain that can only give birth to stillborn ideas,
fed with his blood, his heavy, vitiated blood...

Stop seeing it... As soon as it appears
turn away from it... keep the poor sickly thing
from assuming form...

—What are you thinking about? —Nothing. —Yes, you saw yourself... There you are, cornered... For some time now you seem to me to have a strange look. You look absent, a bit haggard... What's on your mind? —Listen, since you mention it... I'd like to ask you... No, it's completely ridiculous, I'm a fool... —As for that, it's sure. But tell me, what is it? —Well, it's like this... I want you to tell me frankly... But that's too stupid... —Go ahead, just the same, what's wrong? —Well, you're going to make fun of me, but for some time now, I've had the impression... whenever I think... —You think?... A broad smile spreads his jaws... You think? You don't say!... —Don't make fun of me... It's serious, more serious than you believe... Whenever I think... —Excuse my curiosity, whenever you think about what?... —That's just it, it doesn't matter... about anything at all... It's enough for me to have an idea... —An idea, congratulations! It was Einstein, I think, who said: You know, they're very rare, ideas... —Oh, stop, I beg of you... —All right, all right, I'll be serious... So sometimes you get... and it's more than welcome, you'll allow me at least to say that?... you get an idea... But don't look so woebegone... —Yes, I do get one, it amuses me, I like it... —Always modest... —Yes, very modest. I myself don't count... it's only the idea... that's all I think about, I forget myself completely... oh well, you know how it is... —Good; so then what? —Then, all of a sudden I feel as though I were being pulled away... I do what is called take myself to task. I come to... And I... I... I had never noticed it before... I myself am not intelligent... So my idea too, necessarily... and everything about me... everything is contaminated, you understand... —Have you been like that long? —Oh, for some time... —But why all at once? Where did you get that idea? —Which idea? —Why that one, that you're not intelligent. —Oh, that one, as it happens, that didn't come from me... it would have been rather encouraging... since everything I myself think is null and void... Impossible to get me out of it, I'm locked in... You're the only one who can... You're outside... I wouldn't ask anybody else... —What a little cheat you are! You know that I'm like an owl: my own brood is a good one... But no joking, it seems to me, judging from the results... —But you know that's no proof... I have a few gifts... I'm speaking of intelligence. Gifted, that's true, they acknowledged that, but not intelligent... I heard them... —Who, "them?" You know you make me anxious... Where did those voices come from? Who said that?... —No, don't be afraid, I'm not crazy, not completely, I derail perhaps a bit, now and then, but not to that extent... It was real. I heard it with my own ears... when I was out walking with some friends... and they know me very well... I heard my name... I was walking in front of them, they thought I couldn't hear them... One of them said, and none of the others protested...(just: "Ah, you think so? Yes, perhaps so, at bottom..."), he said with such conviction: "He's gifted, that's true, but as regards intelligence, that no, he's not intelligent"... So since then, you understand, I've been a prisoner, I keep thinking about myself... At certain moments, an idea comes to me... it attracts me, it draws me out, I escape in its direction, outside... and then it takes hold of me again: "not intelligent"... my idea shrivels up, everything around me shrinks... it's solitary confinement for life, I'm locked up for life.

He feels a pat on his shoulder... —Come, come, sonny, such things happen at your age... I had critical periods like that when I was an adolescent boy, you'll see, you'll get over it... —You think so? Then it's not true? You don't think that?... —I think you are too taken up with what you are or are not. —But you know, that's new. Before, I never thought about it. I wasn't anything, I was outside, on one side or the other, until the moment when they took possession of me... Now I'm bound hand and foot... —How can you? How is it possible to get into such a state as that... shaking his head, staring in front of him, as though talking to himself... it's really insane to allow yourself to be that impressed by a few poor fools.

40

"A few poor fools"... tit for tat, give tit for tat. Return the ball. Pay them back in their own coin. Turn the tables. That's what it's called. It's also what they call backlash. Many other expressions would no doubt fittingly describe this operation which has been successfully made use of since kindergarten: "You're another!"... The blow rebounds, the aggressor is struck, it's a draw, you separate, calmed down, you move away from each other, your hands in your pockets.

There, the trick worked, all that was needed was to think of it... But not for him, for him to think of it would not have sufficed, there was moreover not the slightest chance that he would think of it. It was necessary for some much stronger person to open his cage, take him by the scruff of the neck, pull him out of there and grabbing the little scamps, lock them up in his place... Look at them, stop being afraid, they can't hurt you any more. They have lost forever their power to do harm... But you absolutely must know how to defend yourself. You must learn to recognize them, you have to hunt them down, don't ever hesitate to grab them as soon as they show the cloven hoof... You see them? They're fools.

What's that? Let's see, it's amazing, it
should be looked at more closely... —Look
more closely at that nonsense? —Nonsense...
Ah no, not that, not nonsense... —Well then,
foolishness, silliness, a stupid, moronic idea...
—No, no, nothing like that, take it away, it's dis-
turbing, it intrudes, it hides everything... things
can't be distinguished any more... Let me examine it... —You must have time to waste...
—Yes, I have, or rather no, it won't be wasted...
One must give absolutely the same opportuni-
ties, greet with the same attention... not spare
one's strength, oneself...

There, I've got it, I'm holding it, bearing
down... It doesn't yield... I keep bearing
down, I am pressing very hard... something is
coming out of it, spurting forth... It's like the

spray of an atomizer... it sprinkles, it covers over, it brings out here, and again there... sort of hardened islets, smeared with a coating of garish colored varnish...

All around things are moving, undulating, melting, changing form, shimmering... warm, foamy waves... They're going to attack that, gnaw on it... spread out everywhere...

Little by little the hardening is gaining ground... Everything is jelling... It's a hermetically closed place, not an opening, not a crack in the walls, I beat against them, I walk around in circles...

Voices with the dull, exasperating tone of automatic answering records keep repeating the same... —The same what? The same stupid things? —No, I wouldn't say that... But I can't stand them any longer, at whatever cost, they must be stopped, drowned out... He is shouting... his voice, as though contaminated, has the same metallic sound, the same petty, dull tone, it repeats like a mechanical instrument: "That's not true. What you say is not true. Not true. Not true. It's a lie. You have only to look about you..." But everything around him is hard, tinselly, closed. On every side, on their jointed necks, heads are nodding... their clacking voices issue from their wide-open mouths... their faces, their eyes are coated with the sly contentment of those who have understood, who know.

Exasperation arouses him, he feels like shaking them, breaking the little records locked in there, which recite, endlessly repeat... But he feels that he has grown stiff, petrified... the words that issue from his mouth seem also to be spoken by a record. They give forth a distant sound like the words we hear spoken around us as we fall off to sleep... "What you say is stupid. It's foolish. Nonsense... It's what fools say."

—There, that's better. You see, if you want to attack that, you can't use your tools, which are much too slight, too fine, they are ineffectual against stupidity...

He comes to, looks around him... What on earth did I do? —Why, you said very wisely, very reasonably, that it was nonsense, silly, that it's what fools say. —Did I say that? —Yes, of course, you said it. You saw that it's impossible to do otherwise. It's the only effective, inexpensive, simple, quick way... We recently had a fine demonstration of this. It should be a lesson to you. It was really—and no mistake—a stroke of genius. One of our teachers, one of the greatest, spotted a sort of limp, slippery idea, he isolated it, he compressed it as he knows how to do, reduced it to a few words, put it between quotes, and without further ado, without an additional touch, without running the risk of getting soiled, without deigning to lose his precious time, he added the simple warning: "fools say"...

But how funny you are... If you could see yourself... your look of astonishment... —Anybody would look like that... But it's a joke, isn't it? He couldn't have said that? —He even put it down in black and white, you could have read it with your own eyes... He got hold of an idea... —What idea? —Oh, I don't remember... some stupid thing... he summed it up and then he simply added on those two words: "fools say." That was all, and believe me, it was enough. But what surprises me, is your surprise... —Yes, I can't get over it... How is it possible? How did he dare take that liberty... —Dare take that liberty? He? But do you know who it is you're talking about? Have you forgotten who he is? He's intelligence in human form. He's the most intelligent of all. Everybody knows that. It knocks your eyes out. There's no use arguing. It's common knowledge, admired throughout the world. Like our finest monuments. Like Notre Dame, the Arc de Triomphe, the Pantheon... And you have the audacity... And you, come to think about it, who are you? I ask you that... —Yes, who? I ask myself that too... and yet no, it's not true, I have always known... I'm nothing... nobody, imagine... a void, a sucking wind... I beg of you, find it, give it to me, let me swallow it down...

45

—What, now? —Why, what he seized upon... that idea... All I need is that, just that, separated from its source... —From what source? —From the transmitting station that he spotted, that he exposed... I want it isolated, in a state of purity... No original sin, no stigma...

No "fools say"... Above all, no. How do people dare? How can they take that liberty? It's a sacrilege. It's low cheating. The dice are loaded. The cards are stacked. By him, out there, do you see him? he's an imposter. He's a swindler. A traitor. He betrayed... —Betrayed? Who? The fools? —No, not them, we're not talking about them. I haven't time to defend them. And besides, they don't exist.

There's laughter on all sides... Do you hear that? Fools don't exist! —Wait... Forget that, there's not a moment to lose, the traitor has caused a terrible threat to be aimed at... at... —For God's sake, at what? —At what's essential... but no matter, you can't understand... All I ask you is to let me have... yes, what they said... let it come to me... Here it's open house, anyone can deposit, without a trace of his identity remaining... not a spot on his reputation... it's like the church steps... Anybody can leave here without incurring any responsibility, no risk of a paternity investigation... it'll be taken care of... hand it to me... yes, the thing about which he declared with that imperturbable cheek of his, without anybody daring to protest... he's so frightening, he creates such an atmosphere of terror... on the subject of which he took the liberty of declaring that people who say that are... excuse me, I can't, it's one of those words I can't bring myself to use... —Oh look at our Holy Willy... they burst out laughing... He doesn't dare blaspheme... Look at him there, with his hand over his mouth: no never... His religion forbids him to say it... —Yes, that's true, my religion. —Well, that's exactly what we were saying: You see his religion forbids him to use sacrilegious words like that: fools... even when speaking of people who say... —Oh yes, who say what?

So here it is. It appears. It's what is called a thought. An idea. An opinion. But what do these names matter? Everything that comes here has the right to the same consideration... Let it come in, settle down...

It stretches out... It takes up all the room... And he senses that a sweetish, sickening odor is spreading... like the odors from sewers, from rotting refuse... —Ah, you see, you're making a face, that nauseates you... Why inhale it, why let oneself be impregnated with it when it is so easy... You can get rid of it in a minute, all that's needed is to do what we do: as soon as it appears, just give it one look and thrust it aside: that's what they think... or rather—think is too good for them—that's what fools say. —No, not at that price, I refuse to pay it. I cannot...

Repress this repulsion in oneself, force oneself to examine it the way people do who analyze spittle, excrement, dissect corpses. But it will more likely make you think of a piece of inferior quality fruit... when you've tasted it, you have the impression that the mucous membranes in your mouth are contracting... How bad it tastes... But there's no question of spitting it out, he forces himself to chew it... while everything inside him seems to be tightening, shrinking... it's poisonous... there's creeping numbness... paralysis... He'd like to rise, call out... but once more, on all sides garishly painted partitions are standing... no exit... he's confined in a hermetically sealed box... he hears excited little cries: Be satisfied, you have been brought to a secret place... Only initiates come in here... he makes an effort to move, to call out...

From far away voices are heard: You allowed yourself to be caught... locked up... You are on their territory... their prisoner... Look at their delighted faces, eyes shining with admiration, with pride, staring at what they have produced,... that hideous trash... You can't

deny it, it's they all right, you recognize them...
To tear yourself away from them, you must...
come now, say it, it's the only way to gain control
over them... Speak the words that will release
you... Repeat after us: That is what fools say.

No, it's that, and that alone, which I must
get rid of... that which spreads out in me and
gives me these sensations... these hallucinations... You see, I'm gathering all my strength,
I clutch it, I hold it close... The partitions are
moving apart... they crackle... they fall...
We are released, outside, in the midst of movement, shimmerings, vibrations, iridescences,
shadings... In the open air. In the fresh air...
where this mummified thing... how, by means
of what sleight of hand, what trickery, did it succeed in usurping the name of idea?... this
mummy is decomposing, disintegrating...
      —Decomposing? Disintegrating? You
hope to make them see that? —Make whom?
—Why, them, of course, the fools... You know
perfectly well that they are still there... you
alone refuse to see them... cosily settled in their
snug box, decorated according to their taste, per-
suaded that they are in secret depths, in the center of everything, from which we are excluded
through our own fault, ignorant, spoofed, led
around by the nose, without realizing it...
      Notice how from all sides, people who re-

semble them come flocking, their name is legion, they stand in tightly serried, jostling crowds before it, this object of devotion... they will weld together around it, protect it, it will become impossible to separate them from it...

Let's hurry, we must have help, we must issue a warning. Take care, don't come near it, this object contains a time bomb... It's too late to defuse it, it must be surrounded with interdictions, with signs on which is written the word "danger"... All who refuse to heed this warning should know what awaits them: they will be fools.

You can believe us, you have no choice, it's a matter of self-defense, not only of self-defense, it's a mortal danger for everybody, for all humanity it is a terrible threat, you dare not hesitate any longer.

Fools. Fools. Poor fools. It's unbelievable. He's the one who just said that. He himself. It was out of his own mouth that there issued those astonishing words: poor fools.

Those people over there, look, I'm pointing them out to you, look carefully at them. You see, they're fools. Here they are. That's how they're called. They are there before us, motionless. They are quite stiff... as though they were lifeless... They are carefully swaddled, wrapped around with narrow strips of cloth, painted masks have been laid over their faces...

But little by little, by dint of watching them so closely... don't you think that you have the sensation... you don't recognize it? It's the same as a while ago... One feels curiously numb, stiff... it's like the first signs of asphyxia in stuffy air, in a hermetically closed place... We were shut in with them... with these mummies... it's a grave, a sarcophagus... and ourselves...

We must tear ourselves away from here, I must return to the place from which you dragged me by means of threats, of terror... I am going back there, follow me, I am there again, come and join me... there where everything lives, stirs, moves, changes form... Here we can't see... —What? Fools? Who do you think we are? Do you think that we don't see the pitfall you have just set for us? That you will succeed in catching us in our own trap? Will you have the audacity to try to make us admit that people who say about others: "They are fools," themselves become... is that it? that's what you want to insinuate, isn't it? that it's we ourselves who are...

—Really, you're driving me to it, you're provoking me, with all that narrow-mindedness, that blindness, that insincerity... I have to take every precaution, force myself not to agree, not to hurl in your face: "Yes, that's true, people who say of others: They're fools... are themselves..." But rest assured, I shan't say it. Saying it makes you feel again, as before, shriveled up, atrophied,

51

suffocating in a sinister place, full of mummified corpses... You see, I was there too. You saw how it happened? That can happen to just anybody... to me as well as to you. You saw it: anybody who has gone so far as to write: "fools say"... you know perfectly that nobody would ever dream, whatever he might do, of calling him too...

They look at each other with alarm... —Oh him! God forbid... Say about him... Whoever was that insane... —Don't worry... not I in any case... And yet he would deserve it... But never, although he had the cheek to say, although he went so far as to write and have printed: "fools say"... never would I stoop to using such methods, to describing him like that...

He must have written these words in a moment of disgust, of rage, when he approached that, when he smelt that dubious odor coming from it... He wanted to keep others from touching it, from being infected by it... like me, a while back, when you gave me such a scare... He wanted to surround with electrified barbed wire, threaten, seize, bully, pillory, designate for opprobrium, expose to jeers all those who appropriate and propagate it... He used imprudent, very dangerous means and, as you saw, he himself ran the risk there, just now, of being caught by me, of being branded with this name... But have no fear, I will not let myself be tempted... there's nothing left that could incite me to set up these scarecrows to frighten sparrows...

He hears derisive laughter, whispering...
—Sparrows? So there exist among us who, according to you, are all equal, all alike, some whom you compare to sparrows? —Oh do excuse me, you're right, I was elsewhere, it was a slip of the tongue, you must forgive me... If we follow that lead, I was one of them, a while back, a frightened sparrow, when you brandished before me, when I let myself be caught, when after the rest... —When you too agreed to say: fools? —Yes, I was that weak... You see nobody is entirely invulnerable... I agreed to set up these dummies so they... —Who "they?" The sparrows? The fools? —Oh no, "they" is just anybody. It's you, or me...

And even... that's what your lamentable tendency to classify, discriminate and segregate leads to... sometimes you are amazed to hear from the mouths of persons you revere as "the most intelligent," things that if you only dared examine them you would call the "most arrant nonsense." Necessarily, since thanks to you "the most intelligent" are in no danger. Nothing can keep them from freely circulating and succeeding in having accepted, whatever they want, whatever comes into their heads... They can allow themselves with impunity to indulge their every fantasy, their wildest ramblings... and God knows they don't deprive themselves of this pleasure... they know perfectly that nothing will incite you to withdraw their privileges once these have been granted for all time... Isn't there, in fact, in anticipation of cases about which it would appear even to you, that what with playing around, they go too far, they really do go beyond all limits... isn't there a specially enacted law that provides them with total immunity: "No one speaks such nonsense as a witty man"?

They look disapproving, grieved... If you are really sincere, if you believe in such perfect equality, if you feel you're like just anybody... on the same level as... forgive us... just any fool, how do you manage to survive, my poor friend? To what unpleasantnesses, what degrading promiscuities must you be exposed... into what traps you must fall... One trembles to think of all that waste of strength, of living substance... When one lacks to that extent an instinct of preservation, of just plain self-awareness, the most elementary dignity, one is seriously infected... You are to be pitied...

Yes, to be pitied. Look at that poor devil.
Watch him holding out to passers-by, going up to
the first person that comes along, holding out to
them in that humble manner... people stop...
What does he want? What is this gadget?
What's it for? And he explains, he gives his
spiel, he touts his line, he wants to make them
accept it... And as you see, there are some who
do feel pity... there are some whose curiosity is
aroused... Look at him, his face lighted up with
hope, his cajoling smile... Come closer, ladies
and gentlemen, you won't be sorry you did so,
take it, take it in your hand... Poor fellow, look
to what a piteous state his folly has led him...
his absurd convictions... you remember?
"We're all alike. Fools don't exist."

—No, they don't exist. Nor is there a poor devil anywhere. That's a product of your imagination... if this prestigious word can be applied to the images that have remained printed on your minds since the days when you used to watch magic lanterns, when you jumped up and down with excitement at marionette shows... Stop behaving like children, quit laughing the way kids do, let's be serious. We're among adults. Look carefully, you'll see...

—Very well, let's look, it may be amusing... Let's see what it is he's showing us... —Oh no, don't say that: not "he"... who's "he"?... it's an unlimited space that can contain no "he"... —Well and good, so it's "shows us" or rather "shows"... Not "us" either, doubtless?... —No, there should be no "us"... the space is infinite... boundless... —Very funny... So this fake "he" approaches this fake "us" and shows... what? What is it?... See here, it's easy to recognize, it's called an "idea"... Where does it come from? Are you the one who invented it? —I? But "I" doesn't exist, I just told you that, you mustn't bother with that... There's no "I" here... no you... For nothing in the world should you allow yourself to be distracted by such futile things... flies that inattentive pupils are trying to catch... you must concentrate on that alone... —On the idea? —Yes, since you insist on giving it a name... You have only to let it enter, unfold...

56

—Oh we, you know, when it's a matter of ideas... For us, all those big names... we're not accustomed to such company, we weren't educated, didn't learn good manners... you know, we weren't brought up, cultivated... So we, what's the use? —But see here, that's not the question... I wasn't either, if that's where you're heading for, I haven't the equipment... a few odds and ends... vague notions... nobody today, that's well known, can pride himself on having accumulated all knowledge, each one of us, as everybody knows, is shut up in his own little narrow field... No, forget what it's called, don't try to find out where it comes from, you have only to let it sink in, let it settle... a germ that can grow in just any soil, such is its vitality, its force... If you let it take root, it will grow, be covered with buds, foliage, put forth ramifications... Don't you sense already that the air around us is more tangy, as though it were purified... this refuse, this foul-smelling decay that you awkwardly tried to lock in, isolate, point out with your "fools say," you see now that it has been destroyed, this time for good, nothing remains of it...

They fall silent. Little sparks light up in their eyes... lighted by satisfaction, admiration... and for them to feel even greater delight, to encourage them, reward them, flatter them, he is willing to designate it by the names he likes to bestow, to confer all its qualifications upon it... You see, this idea, this thought, no longer frightens you... Isn't it a fine one? Isn't it right? Isn't it true? Doesn't it restore complete order?

The little sparks in their eyes are dancing with increased vivacity... like will-o'-the-wisps... neither admiration nor joy has set them alight, his enthusiasm has led him astray... No? You don't like it? It's not right? Not true? You want none of it? They look at one another with a smile of what's called "complicity," a smile out of "the side of your mouth"... —Of course we do, why? But you seem to be in such a hurry, so impatient to impose it... Aren't we a free people?... He raises his hand in protest... Why of course, there's no hurry, we can take our time...

They clear their throats, they clear themselves inside, words are coming out still wrapped in mucus, words that advance with difficulty... —You see, for me, this idea... He looks at it, it's hard for him to recognize it, all wet, stuck together...

What have they thrown over it? He dashes forward to release it, he seizes it... it's all sticky, it's gluey... he himself feels as though he were all stuck together, covered with some repulsive slime... he tries to get a good grip on it, to hold it, but it slips out of his hand, flabby, viscous... —But what is it? What have you done to it? Where did you get that? It isn't you, that's not possible, who spontaneously, naturally, secrete this drool... it's something you've been made to take, some poison you've been made to swallow...

—That's not so, we aren't poisoned, you're the one, my poor fellow, it's you who have allowed yourself to be soaked with it... that's perfectly obvious...

They give each other questioning looks, they nod assent... —I agree with you... Yes, so do I... I must confess that his idea reminded me right away... Ah, you don't like that? You don't like for people to discover such sources in him... —It's not true, they haven't a single feature in common... you must all be blind, deaf... Well, well, blind, deaf... What kind of language is that? It's you who say that? About us... infinities... which no name can embrace... there is no we, no you... —Yes, I was wrong. But a saint... well no, not a saint... nobody could resist it... Listen to me, I beg of you... It's not possible that you don't see... Look at it... it's moving... it's freeing itself... in spite of all the smearing, all the leveling off... it has lost nothing of its freshness, its natural vigor... —It's natural vigor... you don't say... But why insist?... What's the use? How do you expect him to realize it?... He took such pains, he so wanted to make it attractive, irresistible... He dressed it up to suit his taste... dubious at best... he can't help it... I'm like you, I think it appears to be rather crude, it has something a bit showy, a bit common about it... Yes, a certain vulgarity... But he himself, look how he's fidgeting, he's so excited... what's that he's shouting? Ah, Justice and Truth again... Personally, I must say that those words, spoken in that emphatic way... Yes, I too, that makes me blush... Doesn't it you?... Of course it does, but more than anything else, it makes me feel sorry for him, I wouldn't like it if he were made a fool of, he's so weak, so inoffensive... why destroy his illusions?... Come, come, calm yourself, you attach too much importance to our opinion, we don't deserve it... for us, you know, all those lofty ideas... But it can't be helped, he won't give up, he clings to them, hangs on... But just wait, I'll make him let go. Listen, what's the use in insisting? You can see for yourself, you must recognize that we are not equal to it, we're unworthy. Look at us: don't we look narrow-minded? Yes, don't we? He, let's see... they laugh... doesn't he look in something of a daze? Come now, with a little effort you'll see what calm, what freedom... you can forget us, retrieve that cherished idea of yours as it was, with all its qualities intact. It will be enough for you to say it, we won't take offense... ah, it can be seen in your eyes that you already have it on the tip of your tongue... Not so? Of course you have. So say it, stop hesitating... say it once and for all, say that we are fools.

All right. You forced me to do it. I acknowledge the fact: you are fools. And I... I don't deny it, I myself am intelligent.

He repeats the words mechanically, without understanding them very well: Fools.   Intelligent...   The calming effect this produces is like that of swallowing a tranquilizer...   He makes an effort, he's hunting...   But the idea?   where did it go?   What's become of it, the idea that made him accept this dazed state, this disavowal?

Here it is.   They're alone now, just the two of them.   Those who did not appreciate it as it deserves, the fools, have been banished. And he, who is intelligent, he has offered it a worthy dwelling place, a seigneurial palace in which it can feel at home, in an atmosphere of calm, security.

They look at each other: how strong and wholesome you are, how pure, how noble... And you, how powerful, how daring... They cling more and more to each other, they remain together, leaning toward each other, they explore their domain, they advance further and further...

And then, little by little, the idea begins to withdraw, it is moving away, keeping its distance... they can no longer be content, it and he, with this voluptuous intimacy, this prideful solitude for two... It will end by wilting, by wasting away, shut in like that with him... It needs to be seen, to be in the swim... and he understands this, it must go out, take the air, acquire new strength, be admired, sanctioned...[1]

(1) —Readers with even a limited knowledge of French will have recalled that the word *idée* is feminine in that language. The oblivion to the outside world brought on by reflexion on a cherished idea, the masculine-feminine "voluptuous intimacy," with its honeymoon implications, is here, then, a legitimate if daring image. Our own modest, rational language limits use of the feminine pronoun to "the female previously mentioned or implied or easily identified" (Oxford), with the occasional exception of a boat or, even more exceptionally, a train. My translation of this passage suffers in consequence. We can nevertheless let our fancy follow the leader, in this case, the author. *Translator's note.*

He hardly recognizes it... so much time
has elapsed since he ceased to care for it, and he
has never thought of going back to it... But this
is certainly it... and quite evidently it has made
its way, a long way... with what respect it is surrounded, with what pride of having known it from
way back, of being among its intimates, they in-
troduce it... —But you seem surprised, you appear to be quite astonished... He is stammering...
—Why no, not at all... well, yes, a little just the
same... when I remember how, formerly...
when I tried to help it, when I promoted it...
awkwardly, I'll admit, I didn't know at all how to
go about it... with what disdain it was regarded...
people thought it had something common, rather
vulgar about it... They stroke their foreheads...
—When was that? What people? We do not
doubt for a moment your extraordinary mem-

that suffices. You. Just as you are. Just as we like you. With all your incoherences, all your vagaries.

His shouts grow louder: Leave me alone... before it's too late, before you yourselves realize that there has been a mistake... You've seen that, I make blunders, I drink the water in finger bowls... Do you hear what I say? Listen to me... He takes at random whatever is at hand, he seizes a bit of refuse, one of those objects that are thrown out to be picked up with the garbage, and he shows it to them: here's what I like, this is what I cook with my cabbage, nothing attracts me, nothing enchants me more than that... his voice is heavy, wallowing, the words are drawling, he is passing something sticky, repugnant over their faces... But you don't recognize it? you don't remember what he said about that, he whom you so admire: "That's what fools say"? So say it, release me. Banish me. I am an imposter. I am a usurper.

They're in seventh heaven... No doubt about it, today he's at his best, in top form. He can be so obstinate. He can be so prejudiced. Cézanne too was like that. He has opinions that show his background, that peasant stock, it smacks of the soil... If he were not like that, all that sap that is his strength...

He is speaking, the words he has let fly deploy, in his relaxed limbs an extraordinary force is spreading. He leans back. Stretches his legs. Bangs on the table with his fist. He has lost control of himself, he senses nothing... he would never have believed that he could experience that... like years ago when he was a child and it seemed to him that suddenly he had become a giant, that all he would need to do would be to straddle the parapet of the bridge to set foot over there, on the opposite bank, to stretch out his arm and seize the Eiffel Tower which, in his hand, would become one of those reduced models, one of those knick-knacks that tourists buy as souvenirs.

His arm rises, his hand clenches, his fist bangs on the table. He is rolling his globular eyes. They are all watching his large, scarlet face, his thick neck. His voice is raucous: "Up, the dead!" He turns slowly and looks at each one of them with the fixed gaze of a bull. "Up, the dead!" They reel slightly, their tremulous voices sound like bleatings... —But *Maître,* we were talking about deadlines, the demands of journalism... He bangs his fist again, the dishes on the table are vibrating... "Up, the dead! Up, the dead!"... Who budges? who dares to murmur? Appear shocked? —Shocked? But there could be no question of it. —Appear surprised? —Surprised?... Over there, perhaps, that little newcomer only recently admitted... But all of us who know you, we relish it, believe me, we are more than gratified.

He had never experienced, he didn't know that there existed, well-being of this sort... this sensation of being cast in something solid, of ballasting oneself, growing larger, spreading out, constantly held in place, however, by firm, watertight, elastic casings.

It's their combined gaze in his direction that gives him this sense of ease, this freedom of movement, at the same time that it encloses him in the shelter of a form... his own... which they are shaping, which they are caressing... He senses it as being himself, this flesh spread out unembarrassed, shameless, a pinkish flesh becoming heavier at the dewlaps and hanging in folds over his shirt collar, they are his, those big, slightly globular eyes from which something radiates—a strength that makes the others avert their own, stare at the ground... He looks at his huge fist, covered with red hairs, banging on the table... that's his, all that, that's him. He feels like pinching himself to be sure that it's true, he lifts his arm higher, he bangs his fist harder, his voice snaps out: "Up, the dead! Up, the dead!" and their whispers... He's magnificent. A force of nature. An extraordinary temperament...

their eyes, which are gleaming with certainty, admiration, put to flight the trembling, transparent phantom, the ghost that had strayed in among them who are living, flesh-and-blood beings.

In the flesh, proffering himself, spread out among them. May their gaze sleek the delicate skin with silken reflections, of his bald, round skull shining under the lamplight, may it tenderly graze his almond-shaped lids, his slightly blotched cheeks, his thick fist covered with red hairs... may their soft, warm, cascading laughter caress... Why are you laughing? —Oh, because you were so funny... If you could have seen yourself... If you had seen how he looked, that air of mock gravity... Oh yes, that look which he alone can have... —Who's he? —Why, you of course, you, come now, who else could it be? Who has your sense of humor? May I tell them?... Oh yes, tell us, I'd give anything to have seen him, to have been there... You're right, you missed something... Personally, every time I think back on it... We were all embarrassed, it was so bad, awful rubbish... Nobody dared jeopardize his own position by risking a compliment in front of the others... Not a word was spoken... it seemed as if it would never end... The poor woman... Ah well, she got what she deserved, that'll teach her not to subject people to such torture... I think you're being severe, I myself feel sorry for her... In any case, the silence continued... It became unbearable... And all of a sudden, looking very earnest, he said: "How silent we are..." —I said that? I? —You certainly did... How silent... And everybody began to breathe. And the lady was delighted... How silent... with an air of compunction... Yes, an air that spoke reams... He joined in their laughter with an equally fond laugh... —I don't remember... —But how could you expect to remember all your witticisms, your jokes? —But perhaps I was not joking... —Ho, ho, ho, poor woman, we are being spiteful... But that's nothing. The list of his exploits is long. One day... we were in Rome together... —In Rome? —Yes, you remember... when we were young... and the guide... Yes, he has already heard that one, he read that story somewhere, he has forgotten where, it was about someone else... But will he refuse? Is he going to disconcert the person who is so generously offering him... He accepts, he takes in his hand, he looks with affection at the photograph preserved in his parents' album... that young man with the insolent expression, one lock hanging onto his forehead, his disdainful lips, his almond-shaped eyes, his high cheekbones, his delicate head set on his long ungainly body... that's he. That's me. Yes, that's a good one... *Se non è vero*... But it is: *vero*. His body is shaking,

his head is lowered, laughter is stretching his
dewlaps... —Ah, we were silly...

    How cosy we are. How nice it is here.
How safe we feel, shut up in this body. Each one
at home and all together. Good neighbors.
Well-provided house-owners. No need of barri-
ers, of walls bristling with broken glass, no need
of thorny hedges. Each one seated on his own
terrace on the edge of his lawn, listening to the
same chirpings, lending his garden tools, ex-
changing advice, cuttings, seedlings...
    Here is life in the flesh... it plays over
those shiny, smooth, downy, lined, furrowed
faces, stretched or sagging, traversed by tiny
wrinkles, little bluish veins, and those turned-up
or aquiline noses, lips, chins, heavy creased lids,
narrow slits, rounded eyes... their flesh...
his flesh... the slightest attack would make his
spine shiver... would make him immediately
rise to intervene, to protect them...
    His gaze embraces them one after the
other. Gathered about him they give him the
same peaceful sensation that old portraits do...
so true, truer than nature... each one unique.
Fixed in that instant for all eternity. Fragile and
strong. The young and strong roses... firm
lips, downy cheeks... eyes of gold enamel, of
blue china... the unconstrained, consenting
softness of her silky cheek which yields under the

pressure of one's fingers... her hair in which gold and silver strands are mingled... her plump hands resting on her knees between which her soft skirt forms a hollow... Perfect... exactly as she should be. A Nattier. A Boucher... how right they were to overpower, banish the madman, the scoundrel who wanted to tear her away from that...

But it's finished, he accepts, he accepts them all just as they are. He accepts himself just as he is... look at my fist covered like hers with liver spots, traversed with little veins, lying there alive, before you, on the table. Big strong fists that go with strong personalities. My direct gaze which goes deep...

My penetrating eagle eye settles there, on that low forehead under its mass of dark hair... but make no mistake, intelligence shines in those eyes, creeps into the mocking curve of that lip... And then it lights on those big pale round eyes... butter wouldn't melt in his mouth... a look that is too frank, too good to be true, rather underhanded, actually, capable of playing outrageous tricks... This one here, on the other hand, who has in his eyes, in the line of his chin, something shifty, almost deceitful... so frankly shifty that one feels reassured... And that one there, who has nothing shifty about him, so neat and clean one can really have confidence in him... only for certain things however, because he's not very bright, poor dear... no genius... a good guy... but you have to tell it as it is... —A fool? For a moment he weighs the pros and the cons... —Yes... really... A fool... that's the word. A fool... Fools. And why not? —It takes all kinds, doesn't it, to make a world. —What world? —Why the world we all live in... Where you have your place in the sun.

What place? He gives a start... Watch out... what place? You know, I'm going to make you a confession, I am deeply appreciative, touched by your confidence, but the fact is, this place you have so generously attributed to me... I wonder if there hasn't been a misunderstanding... You will remember that when I raised my fist, when I banged on the table, when I rolled my big, globular, bloodshot eyes... it was you, you who were egging me on... an effect of suggestion, hypnosis... As for me, I want you to know that it can't be helped, I couldn't stand it, I escaped from myself, I am once more on the outside... a breath, a shadow, a void in which everything is swallowed up...

They are murmuring: well, well, it's started up again, hold him... —Yes, hold me, yes, all I ask is to be captured, to reintegrate... No, not reintegrate, not here... here I feel that I'm in danger, I came in here by mistake, this is not where I belong, I drink the water in finger bowls... They surround him, they caress his head... —Is it possible to be more charming? "Up, the dead!" shouted savagely embarrasses him, doesn't suit him. He's right, that's not me. Not the him that people know... there's no more tactful, more self-effacing, I would even say more humble... yes, humble... No? Not humble? Humble doesn't suit you? I think I know: proud, rather? You see, proud suits him. A monster of pride... Look how he is relaxing, look at his spoilt child's smile... There, you're all right? There... No need to hunt. It's evident, who doesn't see it? You are that. You are a monster of pride.

His enormous bulk displays his strange shape without regard for rules or regulations... A monster... Of pride... P.R.I.D.E.... An immense banner unfurls, a gold column rears its head skyward.

He stretches his limbs like Gulliver in the land of the Lilliputians, he holds out his leg to set foot on the other bank, he heaves a sigh that causes the mountains to shake, the oceans to billow... Yes, it's true, you must be right... He is holding his hand before his mouth, half-opened by a yawn, he relaxes, he's about to doze off, his sleepy voice is drawling... Yes, you're right, if you look at it more closely, that's what I am: a monster of pride.

—A monster of pride, you think so? Yes, perhaps... since you tell me that the great man himself acknowledges it... But personally, it seems to be hardly probable that excessive pride would be the source of his very spontaneous friendliness, there's no mistaking that, his simplicity, his unfailing kindness... Even kindness is not the word, it is consciousness of absolute equality, it's that look of confidence in his naïve eyes... —Naïve? —Yes, the *Maître* often has the expression of a child... It's one of almost affectionate approval, it attracts you, you plunge, you frolic about... Although I am very shy, I let myself go, I crackle, I sparkle, scintillating words surface in me from deserted regions in which all life had seemed to be extinguished, they form subtle designs, unheard of constructions, which he marvels at...

And then I see something assuming form in him... I don't distinguish very well what it is... but I don't try to, I don't want to see it more clearly, I prefer to leave it vague like the presentiment of a happy surprise... No, I don't know, how do you expect me to know?... —Your ears must have burnt... you should have been there when he spoke of you... —Of me? Really?... a few seconds more of delicious expectation... Of me? —Yes, of you, you should have heard him... he kept paying you compliments... —Oh you're fooling... Not at all. He kept saying: "Remarkable. Witty. Original. Supremely intelligent."

All that and much more, impossible to grasp, spreading over and beyond words, flowing from him to me, causing me to spurt forth scintillating sprays, higher and higher, when suddenly, what's happening?... Is it possible? He looks at his watch... No, not his watch, perhaps not, the thumb and index finger of his right hand come together, give his sleeve a light flick as though to banish, to remove... But does it matter...

In an instant I come to, everything is back in place, I recover my bearings, I've been called to order, I had forgotten my manners, I had let myself go to the point of prolonging the session, I wearied the *Maître's* attention, took advantage

76

of his patience... what was I thinking of?... I straighten up, I rise. —It's time for me to go, I must leave you...

—Leave me? Why? It's not late. Stay a little longer... But now he is rising, his firm look dismisses me, he keeps his distance, he has the air of dignity mingled with resigned resentment, of a person who knows his lowly place and intends to remain in it. Each his own, each at home...

But I no longer have a place, I have no more home... What just happened, that unfortunate movement of my eyes which looked down, of my fingers which came together and gave a little tap to my sleeve, of course, they were my eyes, they were my fingers, but it was what we call a mechanical gesture, at times the body reacts like that with deplorable independence... By affecting you, all at once this movement pulled, tore me away from myself... I need so little, here I am again outside myself, transported into you, fused with you, we are one person, the same warm wave that humiliation spreads submerges us both... Don't leave me, you are tearing me apart, everything can still be made up, effaced, forgotten... Don't go... not now... That was very interesting, I was fascinated by what you were telling me.

But he does not let himself be moved, he

bows with a little smile... Oh you flatter me, you are too kind... A smile that wants to show that his eyes have been opened, he knows with whom he's dealing, he's no longer fooled, useless to try to begin again, after all he's not so simple-minded, so untaught as to let himself be taken in again by the exquisite delicacy, the adorable courtesy of those who are conscious of belonging among "the great"... *noblesse oblige*... the *Roi Soleil* raising his hat to soubrettes... the Lord of the Manor stopping on the village street to converse with a villager: "Keep your cap on, my friend, it's a pretty nasty spring we're having, isn't it?"...

Why too kind? I'm not "too kind." Why did you say that? It's ridiculous. I told you so: there's been a misdeal. There's a mistake in identity. What you are seeing, is a stage Prince, a Rose Queen, a birthday King... it's not even that, it's a decoy, an illusion... I'm like you, impossible to tell us apart, to separate one from the other, we are bound, welded to each other, Siamese twins, don't pull, you're tearing me apart... I'm split in two, quartered, let's remain joined to each other, let's look together, we share the same viewpoint...

We both recognize, don't we? we well know, from having observed them countless times, those meticulous, finicky, always well-groomed types... We've seen them in moments of effusion, of heartrending farewells, of complete spiritual affinity, cast a furtive glance in the mirror, rapidly smooth a stray lock, straighten their necktie, look down at their cuffs, bring together their thumb and index finger and with a light flick remove from their sleeve... we feel the same repulsion, the same need to avoid it...

But what did I do? what happened to me? How on earth, for nothing, for this gesture which means nothing, and which I cannot be judged by, could I have let myself be seized, pushed, thrown in here with these people, shut up in here with these petty, cold-blooded types, I was never one of them, I never had anything in common with them... I was all attention, admiration itself... In fact, I have witnesses whom I can ask to testify, your ears must have burnt, I couldn't compliment you enough... You delighted me, I was drinking in your words, I was engrossed by them, I was imbued with them, when all of a sudden that movement occurred... an instant of absent-mindedness, a slight flagging of sustained attention... —Ah, so that's it, for too long... of effort... —Effort?... Of course, the effort of letting beneficent waves of approval flow from one's eyes, of letting a wide-open silence siphon off, cause to surface, to gush forth from the other, rise higher and higher... so that, at the desired moment, a slight push, a word, a smile, a nod of the head, will give it fresh impetus, keep the stream from deviating, from diminishing in force... just what is needed, no more...

a skilful, experienced gardener knows what care must be given these fragile species... and how happy he is as he watches them grow, come to flower... how he leans over to observe the effect produced...

But what is it now? Where do these gardener, these plant images come from? You and I belonged to the same species... Yes, the same species, like a teacher and his pupil, like a psychiatrist and his patient... each observing the other from where he is seated, the best seat, at the right distance...

This distance—it's all important, we know that well, you and I. Once there, you can go even further... there where the liar stands while he watches how the words he has prudently chosen, judiciously dosed, cleverly coated with intonations of the purest sincerity, the noblest indignation, are progressing in the person he is gulling, when he sees them overcome sudden starts of incredulity, destroy all suspicion...

Further still... there where the poisoner stands as he watches his victim raise grateful eyes in his direction, take from his hands the cup containing the potion into which he has scrupulously, cautiously poured the poison, and raising it to his lips, drink...

Further still... But there is no further, we've reached the end... You see to what point, driven step by step, to what distance from each other, seized with giddiness, we have been swept along... We must retrace our steps, we must meet again, join each other, melt together... —Listen, I wanted to tell you, there's something I wanted to speak to you about, I wanted to ask you, I would have liked to know your opinion...

And he sits down again with a weary, constrained look, he leans against the back of his chair, observing me... Motionless. Silent.

That's fine, it's perfect, it's his turn not to move while watching me hunt, retrieve, lay in front of him... does he like that? No, apparently he doesn't want it... But above all, he should not lose patience, he should not go away, he should give me another chance... —I don't know whether you saw it... I read that quite recently... I believe that it's in line with your thinking, it seems to me that it might be grist for your mill... He purses his lips with an air of doubt... —Ah, you think so? Yes, perhaps... his eyes are blank, he's no longer in the mood...

It's my fault, I made a blunder, I picked up where I had left off, still showing interest in him, showing him how much I appreciated him, when now it was my turn, after what had happened, to speak freely of myself to him, to refer to him, withholding nothing, to lay before him, to charm him, to make him admire... It's all his... nothing is too good... is it good enough?... Ah here it is, I have it... I have it here in a hidden corner, I was jealously keeping it, it's still fragile, hardly formed... For a moment I hesitate... but I can't resist... —You know, I wanted to tell you, I should like to speak to you about it before you leave... I haven't yet breathed a word to anyone... it's not fully ripe... it's an idea that came to me a short time ago... I believe it has... Don't you think that applied to certain facts it would make it possible to compare, to clarify...

My eyes are following it... it is on its way, I see thronging from all sides as it passes and attracted by it, gathering... I give it a little impetus, I can't take my eyes off it... You see, just speaking to you about it gives it form... consistence, thanks to you... —That's very kind of you... but frankly, I must confess... I don't quite follow you... I recognize that it is rather attractive... it's one of those ideas which at first... if you don't examine them closely... yes, very closely... he is straining... his eyes are shining, tiny drops of saliva glisten on his curled lips... he seizes it, he palpates it feverishly, clasps it, crushes it... —No, not that, you're deforming, altering it, you are prejudiced, you have no right, let's be honest...

—Let's be honest?... Ah, you see where that leads to when you renounce your station, your prerogatives, and venture casually like that, without protection, in humble disguise, thinking that you will not be recognized, that you'll be taken for one of my own kind, for my double, my brother... And then as soon as I approach, as soon as I press a little too hard... that withdrawal, those calls to order: "Let's be honest... We're among people who are decent, among decent people, among real gentlemen"... hoping to placate me... But you know, for me, those fine manners, that respect for rules and conventions, when I feel like having fun... why not, now that you have been so imprudent as to unbosom yourself to me, present me your fine idea still intact, in its virgin state... confess that for a beginner, for its first outing, you really could have done better... How do you expect me to resist, it's too good an opportunity... But don't be angry, I've got a right, haven't I? What airs... how he draws himself up, his eyes shooting daggers... in a minute, trampling on all his convictions, he's going to speak out against me, his equal, his peer, one and the same person, tangled together, everybody mingled, identical, princes and paupers alike, without privilege of rank, without Heaven-sent powers...

—What happened to you? You look pale... —I don't dare say, I never will dare tell you... I was seized with such a fit of dizziness... I went to speak, one never should... it was an idea I was particularly fond of... I never can

83

keep... —Ah, I can just see it... Come now, confess, in whom did you confide this time... They look at each other. No doubt about it, he's hopeless... It's unbelievable... To that fool, you went to ask... —A fool? Yes, of course... do you doubt it? I can just see how... he must have lost his mind over it... he didn't believe his ears... —That is to say, it amused him, just to make fun of me... Whereas I, being absorbed by my idea, kept adding one argument to another, I thought he was in good faith... that it sufficed... that I didn't know how to go about it... when I noticed that for him the idea itself... was just a way of putting me... —And you kept on with your little game? —I wasn't playing... he was the one... Finally I was able just the same... I had to make an effort, I took my courage in both hands... I told him to leave... They whistle... —Oh, you don't mean it... told him to leave... But see here, what an improvement... —Not exactly told him... Not the way you think, you know quite well for me that's not possible... I looked down at my wrist and gave a glance, but this time a significant one... at my watch... —Then what? —Then he rose. And to my great satisfaction, he took leave... —Without your feeling any wrench? Without this humiliation making you... —Ah no, I was at a distance, too far off for anything to fall on me. —Well, bravo, my congratulations... so there was no fallout... You were too far off... Far from

84

whom? answer me. —It doesn't matter...
I was far off, I had made a backward leap to protect myself, to protect it, above all it, the idea, to
save it... —So you separated from him. No
more osmosis. You were yourself. He was
himself. Himself, you understand... You're
not obliged to think that he was a fool... —No,
that I couldn't do... —Perhaps then, that he was
a coward, that he was low... —Oh I don't
know... —No, that's too strong, don't force
him, you mustn't be in too much of a hurry...
Tell yourself simply that you were you... —Me?
—All right, tell yourself that he was he. Another
person. Very different... —The way certain ra-
cists say it? "They're not inferior. They're
different"... —Watch out, it's going to take hold
of him again... —No no, don't believe that.
I was given a lesson. I shan't forget it. He's
himself. I'm me. We are we? Ah, yes, I understand: We, but separated from each other,
holding each other by the little finger only...
You are you. They are they.

That's what you feel when the doorman who supervises the exits, after examining your doctor's certificate, gives you a friendly smile, opens the iron gate, shakes hands with you... "Keep up the good work, I'll be seeing you, no, what am I saying? not I'll be seeing you, I hope that this time it'll be goodbye"... and you're on the outside, still a bit dazed, things still look unwonted... but watch out, no more words like unwonted, like strange...

No, everything looks as though it were there for good, in earnest... it all looks unalterable... You're the one who made everything tremble, decompose, they've never moved, they've always stayed where they were, on duty, at everybody's disposal... Electric signs, displays, dress dummies in shopwindows, in gleaming showcases. Under garish café lights, the owner and his lively wife are jesting, passing the time of day with the customers at the bar, as they sip their glasses of red wine, white wine, their whitish-green anisette... Here's how... they look deep into each other's eyes... clink of glasses knocking gently one against the other... prudent touchings, patting jokes, making game... they feel good when they play it... Ah, that makes him blush... We know him, don't we, the good-for-nothing... they laugh the hearty laughter of decent guys, the pealing laughter of strapping young fellows, the thin laughter of little old men... You know yesterday I touched down at eighty... Go on, what are you talking about... you're younger than I am... Younger than you?... Would you like to know what year it was when I quit work? It was, too, absolutely... Kindly smile that adds new creases to his wrinkled face... You don't want to believe me? Listen to me, you can't see any more, put your glasses on, look at me, look at my hands... He's being coquettish, he wants people to tell him... But you know it's true, he still makes a hit with the ladies... A heartbreaker, eh?... You can talk. Well, well, and how about you, it seems a long time... how are things going with you? Still the same old paper work?... Yes, still at it, after all, pretty well have to... Of course, everybody has his own specialty, his own cares, his own sorrows... You look pale, you haven't been sick, have you?... No... Well...

a little... however, it was nothing, nothing to talk about... So much the better, to your good health... Thanks, and here's to yours, looking at you... Come on, I'll stand a round... Oh if that was all... But we're going to have to go home... I'll get a bawling-out... Come on then, supper's ready... How cozy. What extraordinary luck to be here among them. One of them. To talk to one another in nice, round, smooth, warm words that are as calming as the gentle hum of the stove.

They. He. Me. Reflected in their eyes in which nothing wavers. On their faces not a trace of disquiet. They always know who it is there in front of them, raising his glass, clinking it against their own raised glasses... Nice little fellow, not always easygoing, a little too hot-headed, but after all, nobody's perfect... Pretty slip of a girl, a bit too flirtatious for my taste... She, on the other hand, is just the contrary, a real mother-hen... And he, a doting father... More likely they'll drive him to his dotage... Decent old fellow, ah, he wasn't always like that, but old age has softened him... After all, you can't help it, you're as old as your age. As your arteries... And yet she's still so pretty. So well-preserved. Settled in perfect security in the form that's suitable. Fine silver and golden hair. Gentle faded face. Plump hands traversed with little veins, covered with liver spots, resting on her knees between which her downy skirt makes a hollow... Playing the game... What game?

Starting again, are you? It's not a game. She's like that. *Is,* do you understand? You must accept that once and for all. Yes, let's consider that I said nothing. You know perfectly that I have moments of madness, when I lose all sense of what people call reality. Yes. Is... All of us, you may be sure, would prefer to see her as she was. Delicate, rather slender hands. A deliciously rounded face. Skin like rose petals. Thick knot of ash-blond hair. Wasp waist. It was a delight to watch her waltz... But you have to listen to reason. If we listened to you we'd be waltzing around with that little old fellow so bent over that he walks slowly, eyes on the ground... —Yes, precisely, because... Because he is... No, rather because he is not... He's not at all what you see, I assure you... You have only to ask him... —Ask him what? If he feels the way he did at twenty? —No, not that. Just ask him what it is, at the very moment when he is advancing, bent double, what it is that makes him advance, look, there, in front of him... the uneven flagstones, the old pavings between which tufts of grass... gentle, patinated old stones... he knows the shape of each one... you see he has stopped, he is leaning over, he has picked up something, he's holding it in the palm of his hand, he's examining it... now we can try... it's the right moment... —All right, so ask him... But how? How shall I say it? Where shall I look? Which words? Here among you

89

there's no choice. —Take your own... —Impossible, I haven't got any, and if I had they wouldn't succeed... —Then you'll have to be content with ours. They are not bad, you know. For instance, try these: Well, well, Mr. Varenger, how do you do? —No, not that... not "do you do," no, don't laugh... "Feeling fine, aren't we?" would be better.

He raises his head. His face, hardened with age, grows harder... —Feeling fine? You do have some good ones. Feeling fine. I'd like to see you in my place. The mere effort required to stoop down... —Yes, I know, I was just about to say that there, just now, when you were looking at the paving stones, the tufts of grass... when you picked up... He brandishes his cane... —Are you making fun of me? Do I feel fine? I feel fine, you dare say that to me? What have they got in their bellies, those brats? What have they got in their heads? Were they never taught anything? They don't even respect old age, physical handicap, any more. Believe me, it won't be long before you'll understand. You'll see, it'll pass quickly, more quickly than you think, it won't be long before you'll be like me. In the same boat.

Yes, in the same boat. Walking bent over, looking at the tufts of grass between old paving stones yellowed with age, sticking to that... For that alone, accepting... why, just anything... accepting to be bent double, pushed about in a wheelchair... No? Not even that? No more outings even, no more tufts of grass, no more paving stones, just a hospital bed and the smooth, white wall on which at moments through the frosted pane... No, not even a ray... the white cane hits the sidewalk, a fender, a car door... swings back and forth... hunts... all those noises, all those tinklings... not even that... silence... just during that suspended instant, without past or future... just... what? Try to say that to him, to offer him that, if you dare... go on, hand him that, coated with your words, a pretty little gem set in a fine choice piece, hard and polished, the kind that children are made to take in dictation... Ah you don't dare... After all you know your place, at a respectful distance, embarrassed looks filled with deferent compassion...

His back is bending still more, his head with its set features is perturbed by a light pendulum-like motion... —Yes, indeed... his voice has grown softer... yes, that's how it is. You have to see things as they are. The time's not far off... Oh no, don't say that, we're all, you know... every day there are lots of young people... His head draws up, through the shimmering film that covers his eyes pierces an indignant glance... —What? don't say that... You're a good one... There are figures, young man, it's easy to calculate... In fact I am not afraid.

I've been resigned to it for a long time. I've even chosen my place. I know where I'll rest.

His shrunken eyes surrounded by deep circles look at the film that is being shown, with the expression of a satisfied cineast... All those about him, not daring to look elsewhere, are watching it in respectful silence. Slow, stiff gestures. Faces held tight so as not to let their immense sorrow be seen, dribble over... better still, there, on certain set faces streams of tears are flowing without a thought of drying them. He's in the center. Softly lighted by the candles. Nobility. Dignity. Purity. These are communicated to each of those who are now walking past, wholly absorbed in that gesture of the hand which takes the aspergillum and draws in the air... takes the spade from the hand that holds it out, thrusts it downward, raises it, tilts it... granular sound of falling earth... twitter of sparrows, cooing of pigeons... fragrance of freshly turned earth, of flowers... each one like each of the others experiencing the same grave, profound feelings. Each one recognizes them in the eyes that for a second alight absent-mindedly on his own.

Each one sees, nobler and graver than all the others, the young mother in her long black veil, which falls down over her rounded belly... It is as though the eyes that are furtively taking her in, were pulling at the outlines of this belly, making it protrude, yes, more than by the young life that she is carrying in her young loins... just a bit more, without her realizing it... but is it sure that she doesn't feel it?... All of you feel it, don't you? You see what is there... in that line of her belly that sticks out a bit too far, in that back which leans a bit too far backward to be more clearly outlined under her mourning veil... Nobody sees it?... Nobody. Who at such a moment observes things like that? Who dares to lack respect for her who guards coiled up in-side her this sacred trust, our future, our hope, our chance? Who would dare to take that from the fatherless girl beside the grave, deprive her of that sensation?... delicious... how dare you say that?... Well, yes, I do dare... the delicious sensation of being securely enclosed in this form outlined by our deferent, grateful, fond subject eyes gazing at her, so worthy and strong in her mourning veil, who soon will mount the steps of the throne, her delicate throat beneath the weight of the heavy crown, her spine drawn back-ward by the enormous satin train incrusted with emeralds, diamonds. The king is dead, long live the king... None of you would want now to break this tie between us, refuse to take from the one who along with the aspergillum, the spade, holds out the words: "The weeping mother smiled at the newborn babe."

I alone, yes, I'll not take any, hand it to the

others, I break up the circle, I move out of line, I approach the young mother from behind, I seize her by the shoulders and force her to lean back... alone... no more fond, caressing glances... Alone in the world... ready in her turn... asking only to follow, to be identical... entirely alike... You see our hands held one against the other, the same, it's astonishing, one of those miracles... how even the finest detail can be transmitted... you see, each of my fingers facing each one of yours has exactly the same form... one after the other you lift the end of each one of my fingers and press it between your thumb and forefinger, you shake it gently, your voice becomes more highly pitched to resemble my child voice... this little pig went to market, this little pig stayed at home, this little pig bought a basket of eggs, this little pig had none, this little pig cried wee, wee, wee, wee, wee, all the way home... Oh, once more, do it again, papa... His hands, his fingers, his nails, that little crease, that scar that he made on the end of his forefinger to find out what it felt like to cut oneself with a hatchet, little rascal, daredevil, life of the party, young father... after all, how old was he? but how young he still was!... and then, always very dignified, walking with difficulty, but never a word of complaint, stoic till the end, apparently happy, "I'm all right...," when he looked ahead in moments of respite... when he looked at you in a way, you remember? that look he could

have so full of affectionate attention...   —That's
true... , but there were also moments, weren't
there...   his fury, when he flew into a rage, you
remember...   —Oh no, let's not...   —The need
he felt to take hold of you, hug you to him to
communicate to you that coldness, let it infiltrate
you...   to hold you clinging to him, already cold,
hard...   "You'll see, it passes quickly, quicker
than you think"...   No, let's not...   what are you
driving at?   Watch out, you're not going to start
up again?   Of course, who doesn't know it?
he's not of a piece.   Like all of us, he's made of
dissimilar pieces, like many-colored counter-
panes...   no, leave it, let's not touch it.   Leave
to rest in peace.   Leave to rest.   Yes, in peace.

Rest assured, I shan't touch it, may Heaven preserve me from it. When the time comes, you can do your work. I won't disturb you. I'm even going to help you, I'm cleverer than you think. I'm full of good will, quite ready to participate... Let's sit here, on her divan covered with the slightly faded blue velvet that matches the enamel of her eyes... let's lay our rounded palms on the cushions of her hands that are strewn with little gold spots, let's snuggle our faces in the soft folds of her skirt... her fingers caress our necks... Do look at that, look what a state he's in now, my little madcap, my big stupid... What does he want now? What ideas has he got into his head this time? —Nothing, I assure you... But you promised us. Tell us, you tell things so well. Tell us, you who knew him so well, you who had that luck... That's true...

her voice is weak, a weak, slightly tremulous voice, a bit cracked... the right kind of voice for telling tales of a grandmother. Mother Goose tales. You're right, I was lucky. There really was no one like him. I never saw anybody as changeable... he would go from winter to spring, from day to night, in a few seconds. A ray of sunshine, overflowing with gaiety, with enthusiasm... he would amuse himself like a kid and then, all of a sudden, for no apparent reason, you never knew what was the matter with him, what idea had crossed his mind, he would grow gloomy, black clouds began to gather overhead, and there was nothing you could do except to wait for the storm... people made themselves as inconspicuous as possible, hoping that they would be spared... And then the sky would turn blue again, with affectionate teasing, funny stories... the ingenuousness of a child. Humble, at times, when he felt guilty, when he wanted us to forgive him... Nobody could have been more generous in certain cases. Or more tender-hearted. In reality, he was extremely unassuming. Nothing irritated him so much as a gesture of servile submission, of smug admiration... it amused him to frighten bleating sheep, ready to accept just anything... I can see him now, as though he were right in front of me... in the very midst of a conversation... everybody around him was making an effort to shine... one man was relating his experiences as a journalist... And he, who seemed to be listening head down, I can just see his red dewlaps hanging over his stiff white collar, he never wore any other kind... all at once I see him raise his head and with his motionless eyes staring at something in front of him, the way a bull does, he bangs his big, hairy wrestler's fist on the table, and shouts in his raucous voice: "Up, the dead! Up, the dead!" You should have heard the bleatings of all those near him: "But, *Maître*, we were talking about deadlines... a term used in journalism... " he was enormously amused...

And so were we, we laughed, we were in seventh heaven, we poked one another in the ribs, pushed one another about on the bench... Oh tell us some more, about other people, you've known so many of them... funnier still, more amazing ones...

But we can do better, much more exciting construction games, for adults only... Here, to begin with is a daguerreotype... All the features of this face, the line of the lips, the cheeks, the brow, the expression of the eyes, immediately bring to mind in each one of us the word "thinker," the word "poet," and we cling to it. But here now is a page of fine, delicate, serried handwriting that in places is a bit shaky... it is a letter addressed to a pretentious country squire, a Molièresque pen-pusher who at that time was cock-of-the-walk... We see seeping, dripping from every sentence... no need to examine it closely, you recognize it at first glance, toadying, obsequiousness... Mixed with it is a humility that borders on abjection... Ah, but here, watch out, make no mistake, humility won't do... No, let's see, it's not humility, it's clear-sightedness. Yes, icy. Cynicism. Contempt. We might even consider... but unfortunately we can't tarry long over a single item, there are so many... Here is a hastily scrawled note, revealing, however, a real gold mine... one of those treasures that are the pride of private collections and museums... What emanates from it in a thick vapor must be condensed, collected and isolated: persecution mania. Defeatism. Masochism. And here, revealed in this secret confided to his diary, overweening ambition. As well as a liking for official honors. Envy. And in these few words written on the tablet that he always carried with him, don't you see personal vanity?... Personal vanity? Even there?... Alas yes, as though he had known, already foreseen... No, I don't think so... I see in it a certain despair that I should say was authentic... And here, naïve confidence. Conformity... that should be put along with the love of honors, beside envy... And this generosity? To stick to the rules of the game it must be twinned with avarice... which his account book shows...

Here is sadism, that belongs over there, beside masochism. Delicacy... should go here... And this all but mad narcissism... I told you there was personal vanity... No, no... but somewhere there was... Ah, yes, it was in this letter addressed to the chief of the secret police... yes, you see, it is steeped in cowardice... That ought to go here, next to courage... We were obliged to acknowledge that what his intercession shows must undoubtedly be called courage... And here again... what is it? where should this go?... I can't tell any more..., I'm tired, everything is becoming confused, mixed up... spreading out... vast... shapeless... and I on it like an ant... Wait, be patient a bit longer... The game is coming to an end... It's finished. The box is empty. We've used all the pieces. And now you're going to see... But I don't see anything, I'm crawling along, my nose stuck... You must stand up, take your distance... I can't do it... Wait, somebody will help you, you're going to rise... catch that, hold it tight... What is it?... It's the letter to the chief of police... Hold it tight and repeat: I never wrote anything of the sort. I am quite incapable of doing it. It was not I. It was he. Some other person. A stranger. And this note? Could you ever have, even under threat of death?... No, I swear it: never.

But I have no further need of that, I've

been towed, lifted, we're gliding, as in a helicopter, an airplane, and down there, I too can see this form assuming extremely clear outlines... Yes, the higher we go the smaller it becomes, it is condensing, its lines are becoming increasingly clear. It's a formal looking fellow. Cowardly with occasional impulses of bravura. Vain as they come. At times playing the role of a really absurd figure. Erratic. Very lazy. Petty to the point of mania.

Here he is before us as alive as our most intimate friends, as our closest relatives. He walks with an air that is at once obsequious and contemptuous... Suppose he were about to ask you to sit down with him on this café terrace?... May God forbid, I confess I would have to overcome... that's really what I have always fled... but how could I refuse? he arouses low pity... in his eyes there is a begging look... he is so ill-off, he's so alone, poor devil...

Suddenly words, a stanza, one only, it floats, deploys, envelops me, penetrates me... a warm vapor...

And our entire construction, this object so patiently glued together, falls apart... the pieces fitted into one another separate, scatter... they disappear... the words hide them... With all their vowels, their consonants, they stretch, open up, inhale, become saturated, fill up, swell, spread over infinite space, over boundless happinesses...

They are passwords that give access to... words that need only be murmured into my ear for me beatifically to pass over there from whence they came, where they are, in eternal peace, in "the real light."

But who me? There's no more me, no more him; no more separations, no more meltings, there are only their swaying, their vibration, their breathing, their pulsebeats... causing us to vibrate and breathe a single substance, to beat in the rhythm of a single pulse, a single life...

What happened to me? Am I in for another one of my crises? Is it possible that I uttered those groans, those shameless, indecent, ridiculous cries... I blush... How far, no longer able to contain myself, going beyond all limits, did I dare... I who am nothing... Watch out there: danger... I'm nothing. Above all not that. "Nothing" can lead me once more... No. I am... there, I've succeeded... I have recovered myself... thanks to him... I am not he... Not he?... No. Not he. I have recovered my balance. I did not write those letters. Keep that account book. Solicit election to the *Académie.* I did not... yes... it's certainly that... I did not write those words, I did not fit them together in that stanza.   It was he who wrote, on pages of gold...   But if I speak them, weak as I still am, it could seize me again...   I am going to dissolve...   melt...   I will not repeat them. It is enough for me to recall that they are his: what is called "his work."   Secreted by him alone while in his head he was composing, penning with his own hand the most contemptible flattery, the vilest denunciations...   his eyes fixed cunningly on people's faces to see the effect produced...   by what?...   Well, believe it or not, by his boots...   a single pair of which, after patient effort, long meditation, he conceived and had made...   for which he paid...   however stingy he could be...   but he never haggled, never about anything, when it was needed...   when perhaps... with a certain luck...   there, in the reflections of that boot which he was coquettishly dangling, which he was voluptuously contemplating, might appear at last, dawn for the first time...

Who today possesses instruments sufficiently perfected to isolate, collect that substance which at times was secreted in infinitesimal doses by his vulgarest gestures, his most commonplace thoughts, his pettiest obsessions and manias... the exasperating, revolting waste of "what constitutes the worth, the value of every life"...   that moldiness with which he covered himself as though wantonly...   yes, wantonly...

So let's drop all that.   In fact it would be better to proscribe, destroy once and for all those uselessly complicated, stupefying constructions, conceived by ignoramuses for the use of ignoramuses like themselves... all those pieces that have been exhumed, inspected, tagged and classified according to which rules, consigned in which textbooks, taught by which rustic pedagogues?

You must keep your distance. You must keep silent. From now on, you may only approach the statue erected to him on the main square... read his name on the pedestal... raise your eyes and contemplate him as he stands there, proudly erect, arms folded, one lock in the wind, his marble gaze fixed on the far horizon.

How good it makes you feel to sense that you're entirely filled to the brim, running over with what is called Veneration. Admiration. Gratitude.

How good it feels, at a distance, to bow, then draw yourself up with elegance and dignity. Stand to attention. Each one in his place. Each one what he is.

Everybody what they are. Clinging completely to themselves. Entirely justifying their designations and qualifications. Sweet little old women. Exquisite old men walking their dogs with the look of a dog. Lovers embracing on benches. Touching old couples strolling hand in hand. Gratified young mothers and proud young fathers. Children. Birds frisking and twittering. Cats... But cats, when they stand still in full view, hieratic and mysterious... you have to have caught them a hundred times, at the moment when it was impossible for them to know that they were being watched, to be certain that they are not acting like cats, but are, quite simply, cats.

Ordinarily, children arouse no suspicions. They are, quite evidently, real children. Or in any case, if they aren't, they are so gifted, they have been acquiring ever since birth such an admirable technique, that you can watch them day in and day out without thinking for a single second that they "are not," but "feign to be."

And yet, certain of them, less privileged, frailer, impelled no doubt by an excess of awkward zeal, by an unhealthy need of perfection, overplay their roles... are more childlike than nature itself. Too good to be true... Others become distraught, mistake their age... persist in remaining babies... or on the contrary act older than they are, seize upon words they don't know... They are then reprimanded and dubbed as they deserve to be with such names as "little monkey," "little parrot."

Sometimes too it is as though in spite of themselves, from their innocent eyes, from the ingenuous curve of their cheeks, from their lips on which the nipple would seem to have left its shape... something is seeping... it's hard to believe... given the source... and yet it is surely what must be called understanding charged with age-old experience, disillusionment, bitterness, cynicism... But what's the matter? What's got into you? What an idea... Where did you get that one? Look what he has been poking his nose into now... into the stock of things reserved for old people... Put that down this minute, you little scamp, that's not for you.

At times certain adults too give trouble. Too inflexible. Incapable, when the time comes, of giving in as they should, of letting themselves be molded by their newly designated function... They resist piteously, writhe, implore... I understand, I know, it has to be, it can't be avoided, but it's such a shock... there exists perhaps some way of compromising, alleviating... "gray," for instance... "gray" would suit me fine... in fact, you can see, you have only to look at my hair, "gray" fits me like a glove... "gray-dad," but not "grand," I don't want it... not yet... why so soon?... They beg the astonished brats to call them boldly by their first names... they avidly seize upon the children's innocent babble to give themselves childish pet names or occasionally ridiculous nicknames... anything rather than that, anything rather than "granddad."

Others, on the contrary, too sensitive to what filters from the looks that are turned on them, in which they sense respectful sympathy, tactful pity, gluttonously ask for more... they assume advantageous poses, coquettishly take their stand on the brink of the freshly dug hole, with one foot in the grave... Then you have to pull them back and give them a shaking... Hey, hold it, what are you up to? Take your foot out of there, you hear, and behave yourself... If you think we're impressed... I wish I had your toughness... Why, see here, you only have to look at him... No doubt about it, he'll bury us all.

And lovers too, embracing on benches by the river, in public squares, melted into one, "lost in each other"... at times, especially in warm weather, may be noticed, in the long line of their bodies which look as if they were carved in marble, something that is almost imperceptibly moving, something alive... a hand that cautiously, softly, surreptitiously, not to attract attention, like a restive little animal, lets go of the hand that is clasping it, then, afraid, becomes motionless, waits... with cunning stubbornness it starts again... at times it makes so bold as to come to rest on a knee and there, prudently, by means of a very slow rotating motion, it wipes its damp palm on a trouser or a skirt... while the couple, as though this self-willed hand did not belong to it, remains in the same position, as if cast in a single mold, carved from a single block, set there for all eternity.

As if there were nothing. As if nothing had happened. No one the wiser. Above all nothing must budge. Sometimes one single, hardly perceptible movement is enough to upset everything... and precisely this movement, this gesture of a damp hand that lets go, is one that has been spotted, reported... One of our omniscient teachers has seized upon it and recorded it for all time in a book: it's a bad omen, the premonitory sign of a love that is stillborn.

And here now is another gesture, the gesture of that hand... diving into its waistcoat pocket, taking from it a handful of coins, then opening out and holding them spread on its palm... a long time... that grows longer and longer, endless... until finally the fingers of the other hand choose some of the little coins and press them furtively into the outstretched hand of a porter, a doorman, a coachman... who in turn looks down at the meager tip in the hollow of his hand, then raises his eyes and looks hard and long at the back that is moving away... a look from which, as from a pistol, he fires a powerful stream that covers, thickens, hardens the ridiculous, pitiable outlines of a skinflint... Contemptuous smiles, little sneers, head-shaking, shoulder-shrugging, "remarks" quietly exchanged... and then everybody turns away... —Ah, it's not all that...

Not all that, true enough. All that's not for them... How could they suspect... How can they know that this gesture is a sinister sign... that it tolls the bell for Happiness, is the tocsin that predicts the Misfortunes that are going to befall "One Life."

Her life... In her something is tearing, she has a sense of weakness, of cold, the cold of death, while she continues to walk beside him with that look aimed at their backs, emptying at them its load of contemptuous pity... A young

109

couple on their wedding trip... you can tell that right away... a handsome couple on their honeymoon... brand new, freshly cast, perfectly fused... the love poured into them fills every cranny between them, they are one... impossible to separate from each other, to move however slightly to one side... that movement she made when she allowed herself to be carried along by them, when like them, she looked at that hand, as at the hand of a stranger, when she watched it hesitating, choosing lingeringly, holding out, pressing furtively... that tore her in two... a wound that will widen, gape... quick, we must bring together, join the two lips, spread, smear... here's what is needed... thank heaven, she always carries with her a well-fitted kit... here is tenderness, indulgence, gratitude, here's admiration, a bit of humility... ointments of proven efficacy... they are going to disinfect, anesthetize, heal, it won't show... a scratch, a hurt such as can happen to anybody at any moment... there, you won't see a thing... love has sprouted again between them... They are made of the same cloth, cut from the same piece, no separation... he could catch her, her too, when all at once it takes hold of her, when like him, she begins stupidly to haggle... she leans over her open palm on which small change is scattered, she counts, calculates, hesitates... time is passing... while they wait... their gaze settles lengthily, imprints on her an ignominious mark, she's branded... She? but that's not her, can't be her, never her... for nothing on earth could she... rapidly, without looking, she opens her hand and lays on their outstretched palms, she smiles, thanks them, she's always ready to excuse herself... their eyes open wider, their kindly gaze envelops her, may God bless her... she deserves it... generous, sensitive as she is, as she always has been, as everybody took her to be when she used to play unspoiled, pure, airy, free, among her own kind, those with whom one has complete understanding, a sense of togetherness, one's next of kin, one's equals...

But they are far from her, they cannot join her here where she has let herself be brought, where she is locked in for life... here where everything is shut, blocked... the air is close... Thick, inebriating, heady air... she feels enervated, diluted, she's melting, blending, lost in a warm, damp, heavy... And all of a sudden, like the twinge of pain reminding us that the disorder is still there, crouching, that inexorably it is following its course... once more the signal, the fatal sign... that gesture... the same one... a drunkard returns to his glass... but this time even clearer, stronger, added to the other... the hand dangling, hesitating... time passing the way it does in nightmares... finally he chooses, holds out, presses... and quickly turns away... and they looking hard, pitilessly... and she beside them obliged to witness... inca-

pable of doing anything to prevent, stop...
she obliged to see Prince Charming with his curls
hanging in disorder onto his handsome brow...
a real poet's brow... limpid eyes... Sometimes
you have eyes like a child's... become trans-
formed into this skimping, closefisted miser, with
that grim look, those shameful gestures...
contact with him is besmirching, he's dangerous,
he can be contagious... and she is alone with
him, separated for all time from her own people,
they can do nothing for her... Impossible to ask
them for help... to open, merely to half-open...
just a crack, for them to get a peep... What's the
matter? Is it so serious, then? Let's see, let us
take a look... and like the wall paintings in caves
that have been explored, like mummies in dese-
crated tombs, once in contact with the air, with
the light from out-of-doors, this handsome, lov-
ing couple is going to fade, disintegrate...

Above all, no one should come in, the others should stay outside, at a distance... let them
look at us from afar, let them follow us through
their telescopes when we go on one of our outings, when we show ourselves to them... Do you
see us? A transparent capsule protects us...
Inside it you can see two exquisite little figures,
those two dancing sprites... is it possible to
imagine a more charming young couple? the
very picture of love... Watch them run hand in
hand into the waves... how they tease, splash
each other, there, now they are coming out, shak-

ing their dripping hair, laughing, still quite breathless...

Or else, from the places assigned to you as obedient subjects, you can admire us when we display ourselves to you attired in the formal raiments of love, making the ritualistic gestures prescribed by its cult... Our eyes meet, our hands seek each other, join, gently clasp each other, then modestly, as though scared, regretfully part... Suddenly an explosion... as though a bomb were hidden in the luxurious turn-out in which the princely couple was shown. Everything flies into smithereens, is scattered about in loathsome rubble...

That hand dangling, slowly swaying above the small change spread out on the open palm... they too see it, they have seen it, they have been able to observe it at close range, their eyes too have followed, taken in the skimpy form of a deplorable tight-fist... they've seen her, the innocent defenseless girl, led on by him, not daring to turn back toward them, her nearest and dearest, to call on them for help... Stealthily they followed her, they slipped in behind her until they reached the den where she was being sequestered, riveted to him, debased... they carefully inspected the entire place and then left on tiptoe, their eyes filled with tears, weeping over her, her wasted life, her broken heart... Seized with terror, she tears herself away from him... torn in twain, mutilated, gasping for breath, she forces herself to follow them, clings to them, begs them... They should not abandon her, if they'll only come back with her, it doesn't matter, they can come in... they should look even more closely... they should help her to recover, rediscover... there was in him such richness, such real wealth, these should be found... they must remember, they had seen them, they too, like her, they had been dazzled by them... Is it possible that by itself, a single gesture like that one could... they are already ashamed, aren't they, they who are so indulgent, so broad-minded, to have attached such importance to something so petty? Merely to have noticed such a trifle, couldn't this also show pettiness in them? She would blush to confess this to him, he would have every reason to scorn her...

They remain motionless, silent... she seizes their hands, hugs their knees... Just a word, a look, to reassure her, they can still save her... They shake their heads... Alas, my poor child, what can we do about it? What can we do in the face of the rules by which we are governed, precepts founded on wisdom, on experience that harks back to remote Antiquity? This one: you know it well, what's the use in trying to forget it? She stops her ears... Gently, firmly, they remove her hands... You must have the courage to listen: *Ab ungue leonem.*

The latin words resound with the solemnity of a sacred text. *Ab ungue leonem.* By the trace of its claw we shall know the lion... But to translate it like this is diluting it, stretching it out, reducing its potency. *Ab ungue leonem.* By the claw the lion. Nothing between the two terms. One claw and we have the whole lion. One single gesture and there's the entire man. One only, tiny, no bigger than the trace of a claw. We have always been taught to look for it and, through it, to discover...

Great masters have shown us how to go about it. They have furnished us perfect models. We've an embarrassment of riches.

Here, for instance, if any were still needed, is a most admirable example. It's another gesture made by another hand... Unusual, this one is, very strange, so that none of us, probably, has ever had an opportunity of observing one like it. Only a genius, such as God Himself, could have created it... the gesture of that hand holding a fork, pricking it into a piece of food on his plate and instead of putting it into his mouth, he brings it to the level of his eyes, quite close, turns it round and round in the light, lengthily, endlessly hesitating... and from this gesture there appears, grows up around it, rears up with enormous violence, a sickly body, hypocritically bent over, dressed in the livery of a lackey... a repugnant creature the color of mildew... from its rodent's brain, from its ratiocinating mind, there flows, infiltrating everything, an acrid, nauseous

115

stream... its very name fills the air with a stinking odor...

What the hand, choosing the little coins with slow precaution, brought to life before our eyes, is without a possible doubt, a skinflint. Of the worst kind. Sordid. Heartless. Profiteering. He's like that. There's nothing you can do about it.

She raises toward them her face which is streaming with tears... But he is also my beloved. He is the love of my life... So, how... —The poor child is right. How to reconcile... In such situations, there is only one thing to do: put your eyes out... Oh, why resort to such cruel extremes? In very many cases, firmly adjusted blinkers that are never taken off will suffice. They make it possible to skirt with a firm foothold, felicitously to go through... Yes, entire lives... I understand that. But it should have been planned ahead of time, from the very first moment one should have... now it's too late. Once she could see... It happens at any moment, when she least expects it... Happens? Of course, she's so afraid of it that she hunts for it, the way you hunt the criminal under the bed, on all fours, isn't that so, my child?

She hangs her head on her chest which is heaving with sighs... Something must be done, she can't be left like that... These perpetual comings and goings, sudden changes, indecisions and tergiversations, this continual commotion, will end by her becoming the object of punitive sanctions. Steps have to be taken against persons who disturb the peace... You know, my poor child, people like you end up by being interned in insane asylums... Here one must choose: take or leave, love or not love. She raises her head, she murmers: Very well, I'll leave. He is no longer my beloved. This skinflint is a stranger to me...

She's touching... she would so like... she's ready to do anything to feel steady on her feet the way the rest of us do. But she won't succeed. It's going to take hold of her again. Everything is going to start moving again. This skinflint will not stay in place. He's going to move away, be replaced by Prince Charming. Then he'll come back, only to leave again. She has caught her finger in the wheel, her foot in quicksand, she is on the horns of a frightful dilemma... Is there no one present who can furnish her with the means to act?... I can. I think I know a way. It is called "Take the bull by the horns" or "Look things in the face," if you prefer. He's a skinflint. She groans... Oh, just a second longer... wait... —No, my child, you must pull yourself together. Now then, a stout heart! He's a skinflint. Press. Harder. It hurts, it hurts a lot, but that has to be. Print. Engrave. There must not be a waver in the lines. Above all, no more claws, no more furtive tracks. It must be visible at first sight. It must be authoritative. As it is. Steady on its feet. Solid. Unassailable.

Nothing can keep him from letting his hand remain suspended above the small change on his palm as long as he wishes. No look fixed on that palm can force him to close it before the allotted time, then open it halfway suddenly to let fall the entire handful... no weakness, shame, cowardice, no kindness or generosity. He's petty. Selfish. Stingy. For him a cent is a cent. Even if he were rich as Croesus he could never throw a single one out the window. He's made like that, that's how it is... How do you feel, dear child?

The ghost of a smile is etched on her tear-drenched face... It does you good? They're finished, aren't they, those staggers... that sea-sickness... that nausea? You feel as though the ground under your feet were once more paved with cement... —Yes, that's true. But my love... —Why, that's just it, in contact with something neat and solid, through contagion, one's feelings also become... —It won't grow into hostility? —That could be: good, unyielding hostility, that too can have a calming effect... But in your case, rest assured, every tiny bit of your love is going to agglutinate, solidify around this hard block, form a smooth, compact love, "real love"... you know what it's like, nothing can penetrate it, nothing can scratch it... Even though your beloved... —Yes, even though?...

118

I shall always love him? Just as he is? —That's it. Just as he is. But that's what he should be. There have been known to exist frightful assassins, real monsters... real ones, note that, it's important... well, to show themselves as they really were helped enormously to make perfect idols of them, the designated objects of a cult.

doesn't happen to you? —No, that doesn't happen to me, it can't happen to anybody. Not for good. So-and-so is more gifted, that yes. So-and-so is a genius. So-and-so has understanding on this or that subject which I do not possess, I haven't his culture, nor do I possess his knowledge... But to say that he is more intelligent than I am... no, impossible. —He's wonderful. So, tell me: you really believe that you are as intelligent as, shall we say... Descartes? You see, he believes it. Silence means consent. Incredible but true: he really thinks so. It's beginning to be funny... But tell us why, then... What makes you think?... What have you done that would allow you?... —Nothing, I've not done anything. —Look the way he says it, without the least embarrassment, the least shame, he even seems to be proud of it: I've not done anything... He's challenging us... A man of wisdom who holds his head high despite the derision of the ignorant populace... A martyr to the faith... Personally, I don't participate in derision... I don't think it's at all funny. But what are we thinking about? For what are we wasting our time? You see yourself that he's a poor megalomaniac... You're right. He's a megalomaniac who thinks that he's as intelligent as Descartes... What's that he's whispering? "Not more," he says, "not more"... Not more intelligent? He doesn't think he's more intelligent... That's already something, that's a good sign... Not more? Really? Then perhaps less?... No, not less?... that's being too modest... Then "as," like a while ago? No? Not as? That's new. Not as? So what then? What is he shouting, I don't get it... He seems so excited... He's shouting: not more, not less, not as... None of these words suits me... Impossible to apply them to me, they won't stick... "More" won't hold, neither will "as"... That's true, he's right... "Less," either?... —No, nothing... Nothing can't stay attached to nothing... I'm nothing... a vacuum... an air pocket... Infinite. Boundless... And all those around me... like me...

—What is it now? That's no longer him. You hear that strident voice, like a crazy old woman's? "He's right, that's true, nothing can stick to me either, just as soon as it touches me, it comes apart"... Others fall into a trance, it's contagious... Look at them, they're running from every side, in circles... that hysterical laughter, the laughter of lunatics... Peep-o!... catch me... just try it, you won't succeed... I'm a vacuum... an air pocket... infinity... So am I... Me too...

—What's going on? What is all this commotion, this shouting? —Ah, finally, here are the defenders of law and order. It's this one,

you see him? he's the one who made the distur-
bance... He claimed... we thought he was
crazy... he collected around him... there are
always everywhere plenty of over-excited, weak-
minded people... —Come, come... the firm
voice, the calm tone of the men who enforce the
law... What's it all about? Are you the one
who's been talking all this rigamarole to these
good people? —Yes, he wanted to make them
believe... —Believe what? —That he was
above the law. Beyond judgement. A sort of
God. He's infinite. The equal of the greatest...
No, not even their equal, he would feel it was
beneath him to be the equal of anybody whatso-
ever. He's nothing. That is to say, isn't this
so? that he is everything. Everything with a
capital *E*, and that all of us, that each one of us...
we're like him... you can see the effect on some
of them... that's all they need... just imagine,
what a boon, they can't control themselves any
more, and there's no way of controlling them...

Yes, it's a good, gentle, kindly face... the eyes are little windows beyond which limitless space... through which an infinite soul spreads its light... a warm light which makes my words reach toward it, rise, issue from my lips which I do not see, do not feel moving, carried by my voice which I do not hear, words that are formed in me... but why in me, there is no me... that was in the air, it came from everywhere, it came together and penetrated there as elsewhere, no matter... it has germinated, it is growing, putting forth young shoots, sprouts, trying to spread... the entire earth will be covered with it...

The gentle face appears to be hardening, the eyes too have become opaque—a grilled window which suddenly closes with a sharp bang: "Ah, you think so?"

There is a moment of silence, and then the words begin to hammer with precipitated blows: —Why think? Why you? Why do you say that? when you have only to look, it's staring you in the face... It's unbelievable... how, for so long, could people not have known?... when it begs recognition... it's evident... it's absolutely accurate... so true... truth itself.

In the midst of the din made by these great big words, behind the glass something is moving... it opens half way and permits a displeased, frightened glance to come out... —What's the use in insisting? It can't be helped, I don't follow you, I am careful not to, I see where you're trying to lead me: it's a closed domain, reserved for the initiated only, for specialists. I'm not one of them. Neither are you.

Wait, don't try to get out of it, you're wrong, it is not a reserved domain, a forbidden zone, on the contrary, it's open to everybody, to you as well as to me, to any and everybody, it suffices to show a little good will... not even... it suffices not to remain shut in, to look, everything becomes clear... I don't want to believe that you...

His eyes open wider as though to permit the entrance of that which now appears before him: a funny fellow. What we call a strong personality. Intelligent. Esteemed in his own field. Thinks he can do anything he wants, dares to stick his nose... His eyelids narrow, his head is shaking with an air of disapproval —Do you know what you're doing?... Is it possible? You don't realize it?... Listen to me... his head comes closer, leans forward... I have a lot of respect for you, lots of sympathy... Take the advice of a friend: drop it. —Drop it? —Yes. Never repeat to anybody, what you just said. I myself promise you that I'll not say a word about it, I'll make myself forget it... —Thank you. You're too kind... But I don't follow you... —No, really, you don't follow me? You don't see where that will take us? Shall I tell you? That would lead us... if we listened to you... that would bring us... his eyes look heavenward, his lips are moving, they look as though they were murmuring a soft prayer for indulgence, pardon... and then with difficulty, the words come out... That would cause us to do violence... But why force me?... You know it... What's the point in denying it? Who could believe you? Reflect on yourself. Delve deeply into yourself, hunt... When that was growing in you... Don't make that face... Yes, in you. Acknowledge it: it was in you that it germinated, that fine idea. Not in me. You were the favorable soil. You were the privileged spot. It gathered strength in you, spread, proceeded to gain more ground... You wanted the entire

127

earth to be covered with it, you said it yourself. But then one day there rose up on its path... don't deny it... you couldn't help seeing it... Come now, it's coming, it's mounting in you, don't try to repress it... You were faced with... No? You haven't encountered? Why encountered? You had foreseen it, you knew in advance what you were going to encounter... You didn't? it's not that? You wanted it... that's even better, it's really perfect... from the beginning... what a stimulant, that must have increased your strength tenfold... you wanted to do violence... to attack him... Him... You dared... You... But you know, I'm going to tell you something: You are the one that judges...

Stairs that endlessly stretch, wind, descend, mount, descend again and finally abruptly rise to heaven... up to where he is quartered, protected by his dignitaries, his guards... from where they are now observing the man who is crawling, climbing toward him, and who having reached the foot of his throne, where one prostrates oneself without daring to raise one's eyes toward him, has the unheard-of audacity to continue to approach, is preparing to escalate, has now raised his head and is looking eye to eye as between equals... he appears to defy... right away a single telling flick of the finger. "You are the one that judges," makes him topple over, rush, roll downstairs, bumping from one step to the other, a little ball which, at the very bottom, comes to a standstill.

Succession of corridors, high-ceilinged halls of state which must be crossed in order to reach this one where, at one end, half hidden by his long worktable covered with books and papers, audience is granted by him whose name is only spoken in reverently lowered tones, only accompanied by terms that bear witness to unqualified homage rendered him.

If occasionally, in certain cases, there should appear a sort of hesitation, like a slight recoil that might lead one to believe... that could risk arousing suspicion... immediately, the way we touch wood, the way we cross ourselves, they hasten to recite the formulas that will divert from them, ward off... "Why, of course, not for a second—need one insist? —would it occur to me to implicate him. His genius quite evidently is not in question. No, but what on this precise point does leave me a bit perplexed, disturbed, can only come from his clumsy attendants, his unworthy disciples. They are the ones I resent. They betray, they deform, they divert, they conceal. I know, you're right, one must always return to the original texts, one must know how to interpret."

129

But this one here who, without having given any pledge of obedience, without having previously made his devotions, with amazing unawareness, wearing the look of an illuminate guided by voices, is gliding, advancing across the vast spaces of gleaming floor... Let's let him come. We have nothing to fear. Reunited at one bound, welded to one another, our heads helmeted, our breasts protected by shields, we confront him with an insuperable rampart... There he is quite near... within reach of our hands, of our voices... What he is hurling in our direction makes a drumming sound like hailstones as it strikes, rebounds on us, boomerangs on him, hits him hard: "You're the one that judges."

"You're the one that judges."
All at once, in the turn of a wrist, the turn of a phrase, such as they know how to make... No, not in turn. Every word is one more turn in the lock of the jail into which they have thrown me.
"You're the one." You. You. You. No more infinities, no more boundless space. No more means of escape. You: what you already designate, and what you'll be forced to designate when the roll is called, by the word: I. You. And you will straighten up, hands on the seams of your trousers: Yes, me.

"That" which you had rigged up with the pompous name of "thought," with the prestigious name of "truth," "that" which you had hidden under lovely poetic images... the little seed that a breath blew to a certain spot, a tiny part of infinite space which germinated, grew there, which from then on unfurled irresistibly, scattering over the entire earth the exciting fragrance of spring, the welcome shade of summer... "That" is produced by you. "That" is what you secrete. "That" is your distinctive sign, stapled to your identity photograph, to your fingerprint. "That" which made it possible to recognize and arrest you at the moment when you were on the point of attacking... "That" which from now on, will be placed in your file and will make it possible to condemn you: "You are the one that judges."

"You are the one that judges"... we must think hard... all is perhaps not lost, there is perhaps some way out... "You are the one that judges"...

There... is it possible? How is it believable that in spite of their prodigious cleverness, their experience, they could have committed such a blunder?... But watch out, above all don't let it go to your head, run away with you... go easy... yes, it's evident, they made a mistake... They should have been satisfied quite simply with "That judges you."

"That judges you" was perfect. No matter how closely one examines it, impossible to find the slightest crack... But in "You're the one that judges," in "You're the one"... there is what is called a flaw of formulation... Luck, hope of salvation, lie there... "You're the one" reveals, shows clearly, that the "you" is not alone, the "you" has a wrong side, a complement... another facet... Beneath the "You're the one" there is... one sees it immediately... there is: "He is not the one"... You. Not he.

He and I. Impossible to separate us. We are the two points of a comparison. We are the two terms of an equation. We are the two poles of an opposition. He, whom nothing allows us to judge, I whom the slightest thing judges. We have been weighed in the balance. Placed on each dish of the scale. We face each other, he and I.

Of course, I don't see what is here, in place of me. What I do see, on the other hand, there, in front of me, is a man made as I know I am, as we all are, with a torso, two legs, two arms, a head...

Who doesn't know that head? Who hasn't looked at it the way the camera recorded it, the way the film, once and for all caught it... the way it is printed now, I can do nothing about it, on my retina... The way he wanted it to be printed...

Ah, "wanted" startles you... "Wanted" can't be applied to him... "Wanted" doesn't suit him... Not him... But what can be done about it? It's there. "Wanted" is there, so what's the use in protesting? He wanted that "bitter pucker" of his lips, that "deep," "piercing" gaze that heroically plunges, tragically sinks into depths to which never before him... See how he has loaded it, fired it, projected it, aimed it... and how this gaze ends up... no, alas, not on the bottom of the abyss... but prudently, piteously near, quite near in fact, right in our midst, there where in each one of us, has been deposited the standard image, the model of a face that bears the mark, the signs of genius... his gaze settled on that face, it was to that face that he wanted his own to cleave, he wanted to be identified with that face...

—What do you mean by that? What do you dare to insinuate? Why not say it frankly, there exist perfectly simple words with which to say it... "He poses?" That's it, isn't it? He's "a poseur"? —If you like... I'm not afraid of those words... They look at one another... —Not afraid? You hear that? such words as "poseur" don't frighten him... well, what a change, what an improvement... from that, soon, to accepting... —Yes, "poseur" would suit me. But I would even prefer "full of his own importance," an excellent expression which would allow me more closely to approach... Yes. Full. Brimming over with himself. Unable to leave himself. Fascinated by the image of himself that he projects. Preoccupied by that more than by anything else. Caring first for that. There's the be-all and end-all. There is the fountainhead. A polluted fountain. Everything that flows from it is contaminated... all his "discoveries," his ideas... Wait, don't move, only one second more... Here are further proofs of this... Here are documents, intimate conversations, letters, personal diaries in which he was imprudent enough to reveal... Don't turn away, try to overcome your... I know, I feel it too, when I rummage, when I ferret about like this, a repulsion... but you have to... please look... here's what he wrote with his own hand, in black and white, to his mother, to his fiancée: "At whatever cost, I must find something that will make me famous"... And here's what he scrawled in one of his notebooks: "I want to be rich. Powerful. I want to construct a world from which no one can escape... in which I shall imprison them all"... And then he set out to seek...

Whispers, subtle titters slip by...

—To seek? Why that's admirable... To seek... thank goodness... fortunately for us... Smiling heads are nodding assent... Yes, thank goodness... Only those who seek...

There's nothing like it for finding...

—But he "found" nothing... There was nothing there... there was no conglomeration, no condensation... nothing toward which he strained, to which he felt dedicated... not even dedicated... which should have held him, absorbed him entirely, drained the last drop from him without his realizing it, in spite of himself... But he, cold-bloodedly, out of nothing, everything was usable, just any sham, any false truth, provided it permitted him to fabricate that showy, peremptory, ponderous product of his, which applied to every living thing... And remember the anathema that this "seeker" hurled at those who tried to be of use to his "discoveries," who brought grist to his mill... but they brought too much, they did it too well... and what if they were going to divert to themselves, take from him... him, him, him...

But you know that, you see it too, don't you? It knocks your eyes out... No? It doesn't knock your eyes? That either? Or that?

I hover about him, I leap, I bite, I tear off bits and shreds, a sickening odor comes from them, a sticky liquid is dripping on me...

Now I can't break away from him, I stick to him, I weigh upon him, I clasp him to me, I am the recipient of his breath, his sweat, his blood, we are interlocked, mingled together in a repel-

135

lent hand-to-hand struggle... What happened, then?... How did we come to that? I don't remember what cause I am fighting for... What idea. Was there one? I no longer know, all I do know is that at the stage where I now am, either he or I must win. I grip him with all my might, more and more I sink into something soft that yields for a moment and then reassumes form, I am caught in its toils...

They should come to my assistance, they alone can rescue me, which they well know... one sign from them, a single little sign of support, of acquiescence, would suffice to weight the balance in my favor... I cast imploring glances in their direction...

In their attentive eyes, in their silence, images, words file by... mongrel barking at passers-by, dogs bark, the caravan passes, a louse in the lion's mane, the frog and the ox... and I leap and I yelp and I bite and I swell...

But it's a lure, an illusion. Nothing that comes from him is reflected in them, he projects no image in them, they do not look at him, they would be dazzled, blinded... what they see, is a mongrel that doesn't recognize his own reflection in the mirror, and barks and leaps and bumps himself, becoming more and more furious, and trying comically to bite... A mental deficient inveighing and threatening... not

God, of course, as he thinks he's doing... Ah, it really can be said of him that he made God in his own image... it's really against that image, the image of himself, that he is so dead set... Look at him, watch him, with what hatred he attacks what he is, his own petty tricks, his sordid calculations, his rancors, his ambition, his pretentiousness, his pose... A fine self-portrait...

Naturally, the poor thing can't see beyond the end of his own nose.

In such circumstances, when you've reached so extreme a point, when you've got yourself into such a bad fix, when you've made such a dangerous blunder, when you've been had like a rat, you really don't know to which saint you should pray.

But now all of a sudden, before he was even called upon, the saint appears... A heavenly apparition... His emaciated body floats in over-large garments, his feet are shod with canvas sandals such as he always wears, his disheveled white curls float like an aureole above his nobly lined face, innocence radiates from his childlike eyes... in his far-off gaze it would be impossible ever to discover the slightest movement in the direction of those who are watching him... Quite simply, he doesn't see them, since he can't see himself being absent as he is, from

137

himself, yes, constantly absent-minded, you remember how he stared at the egg he was holding
in his hand while his watch was cooking in boiling
water... He's my savior, my redeemer... it
sufficed for him to appear and here I am suddenly
released... When I look beyond the end of my
nose, he's the one I see... No, what am I saying?
not the end, of course... far from the end and
higher up... I am aware of distances... I know
how to measure grandeur, pre-eminence...
I know how to admire, I can even adore...
You can see a beatific smile stretching across my
face... fondness softens my voice as I point him
out to you... —Ah that one, he really is something else again... —You can say that his idea
possesses him... He belongs to it entirely...
He is a pure man. He's real.

A hand gently taps me on the shoulder...
—How right, how sane that is. We'll admit that
we weren't very nice, we put you in your place
rather harshly, it was so exasperating, all those
attacks, that impertinence, but one is obliged to
recognize that you have made great progress, a
big step forward on the road to reason, to submit-
ting to what is evident.
You have finally understood like everybody else that there can be no idea without its
master. And it is rare that a misplaced idea is
brought to the Lost-and-Found office, rarer still

that it remains there.   It is also rare that the person who perceives that he has been robbed of an idea doesn't trumpet this fact far and near. It can even happen, in the case of highly prized ideas, that nations dispute over their ownership, each one maintaining that one of its citizens holds the legitimate rights to the title.

So you have understood that to attack an idea, it's a good thing to go back to the one who owns it, who derives from it and from whom it derives, to trace it in photographs, portraits, intimate diaries, notebooks and letters.   And on the other hand, if an idea that has force...   a force, let it be said in passing, in which like ourselves, poor ignoramuses that we are, you are often obliged to believe simply on the faith of what connoisseurs, specialists say about it...   Yes, you know that an idea communicates its brilliance to disheveled hair, canvas sandals, eggs and watches, and that in turn its own brilliance is enhanced...

Are you sure that the great man you so venerate, as indeed we all do, was as unconscious of this fact as you think?   Do you believe that he could have been totally unaware of the amount of charm that these attributes, as you have shown, conferred upon his idea?

As regards our own great man, although it is true that there was something "intentional," "posed" about him, it is probably because he had the misfortune to have been caught off his guard...

139

He was taken by surprise at one of those moments—there are bound to be a few, even in the case of someone like him—when suddenly the idea deserted him... then, to do what he should by it, to compensate for its absence, he was obliged to pay with his person... although he was quite burnt out, he had to hastily fabricate for himself a mask of genius, on the current model, etch in a bitter pucker... project as far as he could... not very far needless to say, under the circumstances... a "deep" look... Our two great men are perhaps not as different as it may seem to you. They are all the same more complicated than you think. Isn't that funny? Now we are the ones who must tell you this...

Ah, those independent spirits, those recalcitrant figures, those insubordinates, when they fall back in line, are often more submissive and zealous than the others... In fact this one, I always thought he would, gave promise of becoming an excellent fellow. —Would you believe it, I once caught him in front of a newsstand, taking a sneaking look at the picture—the one of their happiness—of a royal couple... or was it a neglected queen?... Come now, don't blush, which of us can boast in all sincerity of never having succumbed to temptations that strong? Well and good, let's not insist, let's not quibble too much, not reproach him with his tendency to oversimplify, his naïveté... Better too much simplicity, too much ingenuousness, than that sort of destructive attitude, that cynicism.

But let's forget all that. Besides, he admits, doesn't he, that he was dragged into it, he no longer knew what he was doing when he so stupidly attacked... it's better not to think about it any more... he had been so frightened, "You are the one that judges" hurled at him all of a sudden had blinded him for the moment, made him lose his head... Yes, his head, he had lost it. But now he has found it again, hasn't he? And he has every reason to be satisfied, because it must be said that, all the same, it is an excellent head... All right, all right, let's not grow sentimental, all's well that ends well. I even have a nice surprise for you... Do you know what somebody said to me about you? No? You don't know? Well, you big crazy, I was told that you are somebody. —Somebody? Me? —Ah, isn't it so, to be able to say "me," to be yourself, that's already a good thing. But it's even better than that, it's very fortunate to be able to say to yourself that you're somebody. So you want to know who... you're right, if it had been said to me by a fool... but I would not have repeated it to you... No, the person who said it to me... You'll agree that he... Yes, that I'll agree... You agree that he is somebody...

—Of course... And since you speak to me of him, I shall say that he even wrote me... a very fine letter, I kept it... he had been one of the persons who thought that an idea of mine...

there were several in fact... he hears a sort of hardly perceptible murmur, like a very faint echo... several... several somebodies... They nod assent... —You see... That's fine... —Yes, several... You know their standing, what they represent... But since you're interested, they have given me proof... at times even too flattering... —Not at all, why too flattering? Don't be so modest... That reminds me, did he write you?... He also wrote to a young friend of mine. He writes a lot. If one of these days his letters were published... although to tell the truth, I don't think so... And this one also wrote you? He didn't? told you... Well, that's good... there's a sort of movement among them, it's as though they were restraining their feet which, in spite of their efforts, are stretching forward to give him, who is leaning toward them, prostrate before them, a tiny little kick... the vague suggestion of a movement that sends a very light wave through him... a light current of fear runs through him... suppose, later on, when he's alone, at night, lying in bed, he had lost his outlines, started to stretch, to spread out, become enormous again, an ocean... and suppose then that the tiny little wave which like him was swelling out of all proportion, started rolling inside him in enormous billows, if cyclones should rage in him, if typhoons should blow up... But all is calm. Their feet are dangling peacefully, they are looking at him as he stands there in front of them, very dignified. Aware of his worth. Appreciated by some of the best. Deserving to be one of those to whom may be applied these words that ballast them, that make them stand up straight on their two feet: "He's somebody."

Finally a little wisdom, a little order in this nice big head... and now he has become what I always thought he would... I always had that presentiment, my little finger told me so, these are things about which I am rarely wrong... I knew that the day would come... yes, you'll see, you'll be somebody one of these days, my crazy little boy, my big stupid... My head is lying on her knees and I turn it from side to side to feel the soft, silky cushion of her palm glide over my ear, my cheek... I raise my head to gaze at her fluffy white shawl, her fine silver and golden hair, her rosy face, furrowed with little wrinkles, the reflections of her faded enamel eyes... A perfect receptacle, a crystal scent-bottle entirely filled with deliciously perfumed ingredients that we call: Tenderness. Pure love. Detachment. Serenity. Courage. Pride. Inborn wisdom...

144

—Intelligence? —Oh no, not that... above all, no... —How's that? Don't tell me that your grandmother was... —Oh no, she was no fool, believe me, she was far from it. She was far from all that, stupidity, intelligence... she was elsewhere, on this side and that... I couldn't imagine... I never gave it a thought, that seemed to be taken for granted... but since you mention it, yes, it's true, I don't imagine that for her, ideas could upset, besmirch... disturb by their contortions, convulsions, grovelings, sudden starts, leaps... push one another out, impatient, avid, quarrelsome as they are... that they could show up in her eyes, insinuate in them their own febrile gleam... perforate the reassuring opacity of that faded enamel, its gentle reflections, on the tip of a searching, ferreting, piercing gaze... And besides, if ever by some misfortune, by the most improbable, unbelievable of chances an idea should be born to her, one would be seized with pity at the thought of its fate, of the obstacles that the poor darling would inevitably encounter, handicapped as it would be by its birth.

No, no, how can you accept for a single instant, you who taught me... but you surely wanted to test me... I know that here everything should be just where it belongs, in a perfectly appropriate receptacle.

She is one of the most perfect, she in

whom everywhere, in the slack line of her rosy cheek, in the reflections of her enamel eyes, in the folds of her soft skirt, in the little veins of her plump hands, one sees dawning, sparkling love, innocence, kindness, serenity, wisdom...

As regards intelligence... there are more suitable receptacles for intelligence, and which are also perfect. This one, for instance... But why "for instance?" as though it were one among others... whereas it is unique of its kind. Like her an absolute. A model. Her equal in perfection, in plenitude. They match each other.

He is so entirely filled with intelligence that people end by mistaking them for each other, intelligence and him. Who has not heard people say of him that he *is* intelligence itself?

But who am I to judge of this? Although my place is not, far from it, at the very bottom of the ladder on which he occupies the top, since, as you yourselves said, I am nobody. But between those who are somebody and him—what a distance... How many stairs that stretch, wind, descend, reascend and finally lead directly to heaven... what reaches of slippery floors to arrive at the place where he has his quarters, he in whom ideas form, come together, bloom in a perpetual fermentation and emulsion... their force, his immense force, propels them... very far, further and further... to a point at which one would never have imagined... —Into her own domain? —No, after all. Not that far. There he stops on the threshold, removes his hat. Remember the pictures that showed him coming to pay her a visit, as from time to time duty, affection and reverence incite him to do. Doesn't he look almost naïve, as though he had become a little boy again? With what devoutness he listens to her, with what humility he bows as though to receive her benediction... Which of us watching them did not feel moved to tears?

No, but sometimes the powerful impulse of his intelligence can lead him to overleap certain bounds... He audaciously worms his way into places where nobody, ever, before him, even into the most exclusive, the most sanctified spheres, where each individual supposed that a man's house was his castle...

How could I do it? I still don't understand how, forgetting who I am, I, myself, dared proceed to the place where he alone... yes, I see quite well, when I was pushing my little idea in front of me, I reminded people of a little insect pushing his tiny food ball in front of him, lifting it with difficulty... forcing myself to go on, trying to climb up his giant toe, the enormous thumb of his foot...

A single little movement on his part and I

147

was bowled over, lying on my back, pulled back-
ward and held flat on the ground by the heavy
shell of the fools... a fool trying piteously to
turn over, to stand up, and unable to do anything
but kick his legs about, churn the air with his tiny
paws...

Now under the effect of the rays he emits,
I see how everything around me is arranged—
each person and each thing in its right place...
all the scattered pieces among which out there
the others feel their way, stumble, here meet,
dovetail with absolute precision. No disorder.
Not a crack.

If ever anybody should see—but who has
such eyesight as that?—anything like a fissure taking place, those who have deserved to look after
the reserves, the inexhaustible resources that he
has accumulated for us, would immediately discover, by extracting that which, once it is well
mixed, crushed, sifted, purified, would permit
them to fill in, smooth... you can be certain that
it would not take long for everything to be once
more in perfect order...

Everywhere... in me as well... I who
stay exactly in my place and have no desire to
budge from it, I open to allow to enter, to settle,
to illuminate, to collect in me and cause to dovetail, to weld... so that I too, clean, all smooth...
nothing sprouting... no, nothing, but if ever

again, something inside me started... how could I? who am I? Not who am I, just like that, no, have no fear, you realize perfectly that I know who I am, I know who he is... No, I meant to say: who am I to be able, I, with only my limited resources... But you are all there, near me... and you will see it right away, what, in spite of myself... and you will help me, you will examine it, you will cut it down to size, you will call it what that deserves to be called and you'll put it in its place, you'll put me back in my place, you'll put everything in order again, of that I'm sure... but what am I thinking of? What excessive scruples, what inordinate need of security.

What's going on? You'd think... didn't
you notice it?...   It seems to me that I sensed...
In what he said?...   No, it's more in his silence...
when he was listening to us I felt, I should not
have been surprised if there had issued from his
lips... —Oh no, what will you imagine next?
It was nothing...   I was elsewhere...   the most I
could have done would have been to repeat without thinking what I was saying...   Others said
that first, not I...   others who have proved that
they were not...   but who does not have such
moments? He himself perhaps...   —What did
you say? Who are you talking about?...   —No,
not about him, of course...   but I just wanted to
point out that none of us is totally preserved
from... We should be forgiven... One moment
of vacuity, of inattention, is not enough for...

—Oh, yes it is. There's many a case in which almost nothing... where there's smoke there's fire... sufficed to mark an entire life... —Yes, I know, but I... —What do you mean you? Nobody, you know that, even among "somebodies," can enjoy complete immunity when it's a matter of... —But I, what I meant to say... No, what am I talking about? I didn't mean to say anything... —Ah, you see, you're hesitating, spluttering, I was not wrong... you can thank me. I stopped you in time... I sensed, I never mistake it... there was in your expression, in your silence, yes... a sort of reticence... a second more... with the devil at your elbow... and words were going to come out...

—No, not I, I couldn't say anything, for the simple reason that I hadn't thought anything. No, I assure you, not spoken by me... I, what words?... Why, I'm surprised... After all, what are those words? Where did you get them? How did they come into your mind? —Oh I don't know... I must have heard... —Heard where? From whom? —I forget... —Think. That's serious, because if you did not hear them... Well... So speak them then, those words that you imagined, that you "felt" forming in me, rising to my lips... All right, all right, let's not insist... This time it will not be chalked up against you... You believed, just believed you perceived, that's what is a bit awkward... yes, it was an hallucination...   but you must watch yourself, that's disquieting...   You know quite well what that is, what you imagined, what you believed you heard: That's what fools say.

DATE DUE

MAY 24 '77			
MAY 2 '78			
39 505 JOSTEN'S			